WHERE THE PELICAN FLIES

Marilyn Martinuzzi

WHERE THE PELICAN FLIES

Copyright © Marilyn Martinuzzi 2011

ISBN 978-1-4475-9222-8

Cover design and computer layout: Steve Martinuzzi

Paperback

Printed online by Lulu

ABOUT THE AUTHOR

Marilyn Martinuzzi is a recently retired primary school teacher who has always been an avid reader. She thrived on literature studies at school, teachers' college and university. After many busy years as a mother and teacher, she has now found more time to write,  completing many short stories and poems, and joining two writers' groups, Beerwah Writers' Group and The Society of Women Writers in Queensland. "Where the Pelican Flies" is her third book.

Marilyn lives at Caloundra on Queensland's Sunshine Coast. She has three grown up children who are all married, and one delightful granddaughter.

When she is not writing, Marilyn loves spending time with her wonderful family, reading, doing arts and craft and walking on the beach.

For

Matthew and Sam, Daniel, Brooke and Sienna,

Anna, Kurt and baby,

With love always.

ONE

It was Monday, her usual day off work, and this was her sanctuary, a place where she could be alone with her thoughts. Jasmine sat on the rock wall, knees up to her chin, and gazed over the tranquil waters of the Passage. A few wispy clouds scudded across the azure sky, and a soft breeze skipped over the ripples, and parted and flipped her hair. Several small fishing boats bobbed listlessly out in the channel and seagulls squealed and dipped near the jetty, where groups of people were walking and fishing. She breathed in the salt and seaweed, willing the sea air to spread through her body, rejuvenating it, healing it.

Moving from Sydney had been unsettling. She'd left her friends, her old home, memories, a big chunk of her childhood. And Scott. They'd met a few years ago through mutual friends they had back in Sydney. Theirs was a long distance relationship because Scott had a secure job in Sydney and she was now settled in Queensland. They got together every few weeks whenever they could, but both of them knew deep down it would never work. She still thought about him, how he'd cheated on her. How could she trust anyone again after all those lies? The hurt ate away at her soul. She sometimes felt like crawling into a cave and never coming out.

It's not that she was unhappy here. She'd always loved the coast when she came up on holidays, and she had made some special friends. But she was restless, anxious. She needed to break free, make it on her own. She was nearly twenty-two for God's sake. But every time she mentioned it, a veil fell over her mother's face and then came the guilt. They'd supported each other through the rough times, so how could she just up and leave? And could she afford to leave home anyhow? She wondered how things might have been different if her dad was still around. It wouldn't be a struggle financially, but he was on his own journey and his family didn't figure in it.

She was only vaguely aware of the activity around the boat ramp nearby where boats and fishermen were coming and going at scattered intervals. She was watching a group of pelicans who were huddled below her on the sandy beach. There were about six of them, some stretching their wings, others waddling casually, their heads and bills moving up and down, continually on the lookout for food.

More pelicans came gliding in on her left, their focus a young fisherman approaching the filleting table with his bucket. He wore typical fisherman clothes, grubby shorts and a flannel shirt. His head was a mass of dark curls, but it was his physique her eyes were drawn to. Strong broad shoulders, thick arms, tanned skin. What a hunk. He seemed oblivious to his surroundings, focussing on the task at hand. He threw the last of the fish scraps to the mass of snapping bills, washed his hands and walked off.

'Hey,' Jasmine yelled at his retreating back. 'You've forgotten something.' She indicated the plastic bag he'd left on the filleting table. It was flapping in the breeze, its smelly contents of left-over bait anchoring it tentatively until the next gust of wind dislodged it. He stopped beside his black ute, the dripping tinnie already attached to the trailer. He spun around presenting an angry, unshaven face.

'What?' he glared.

'Your rubbish. Get rid of it. It would be a slow death if one of these pelicans swallowed it.'

'Who do you think you are? Go jump.' He slid into the ute and drove off, the trailer jumping and protesting over the uneven road surface.

God, what a moron. It's people like him who care only about themselves and don't give a fig about the animals or the environment. They're the big problem. She shook her head and walked over to the table. She held her breath, grimaced and picked up the offensive-smelling bag with two pinched fingers. The pelicans waddled towards her, jostling and grunting, their scissor bills open and snapping.

'No guys. You wouldn't like this,' she said as she walked off to dispose of the bag. She washed her hands and returned to a wooden park bench overlooking the silver waters. This was Pumicestone Passage, a narrow stretch of water and sandbank ridges separating mainland Caloundra and Golden Beach, where she was now, from the northern tip of Bribie Island.

The entire channel of water was 35 kilometres long, stretching from the populated southern end of Bribie to the narrow point at the north at Caloundra. The neck was just low sand dunes covered with she-oaks and coastal shrubs which provided a buffer from the pounding surf of the Pacific Ocean on the eastern shores. Some locals were concerned that the ocean might break through one day and they made dire predictions about the impact this would have on the homes built close to the waterway as well as the many holiday units hugging the shores. But Jasmine had seen photos her grandfather had, and the tip of Bribie looked much the same years ago when he fished around there. Pumicestone Passage got its name from Pumicestone Creek named by the explorer Matthew Flinders when he found pieces of pumice stone washed up on the sandy edges of the channel. The volcanic activity in the area millions of years ago sent lava spewing out of the earth leaving behind stark volcanic plugs rising from the coastal plain to the west of Caloundra. These eerie crags of rock called the Glass House Mountains provided a stunning backdrop as the sun slipped away at the day's end.

When Jasmine was here with the pelicans she thought of her grandfather, a fisherman working out of Happy Valley, who knew the passage in all its moods. She smiled as she remembered coming up on holidays and going fishing with him in his boat. They would often pull the small boat up on Bribie's northern tip and picnic under the shady bushes. He told her stories of the old days and pointed out interesting things, the names of the trees, and the many birds; the plovers, oystercatchers, godwits, tattlers and the migratory terns. She couldn't believe some of these small birds would travel so far, starting their journey on the Asian continent, then flying all the way here to the Caloundra sandbanks. There were so many sandbanks that at low tide you could almost walk from one side of the channel to the other. She and her grandfather would wade out searching for yabbies and worms. Often she would lie back in the sand and gaze at the pelicans drifting in the air streams. She loved watching the pelicans' bumbling landings, their wings spread wide, their webbed feet splayed out like water skis, and the rhinestone spray as they hit the water.

'You know Grandpa, one day I'll be a pelican. I'll be free like them,' she'd said.

'Yep, this is their place alright,' Grandpa smiled, looking up into the sky. 'Maybe one of them is Mr. Percival.'

'And maybe I can have one for a pet just like him. And I'd teach him tricks.' Grandpa had read her the story about Mr.

Percival. It was called "Storm Boy", the tale of a boy's friendship with a very special pelican.

She'd loved these birds ever since, painting and drawing pictures of them and collecting figurines. There was even a small pelican tattoo gracing her ankle which she'd had done on her sixteenth birthday, much to her mother's despair.

And here she was now, camera around her neck with an audience of pelicans. This area around the boat ramp was one of their favourite haunts and they assembled like old men at a meeting. Jasmine focussed her camera on a group bobbing in the shallows and zoomed in. Later she would put the photos on her laptop and use them for the inspiration and composition of her paintings. As an artist she was attuned to the shapes, textures and colours in nature. When she first painted the pelicans she realised that their plumage was not really white and black. In fact she didn't use black paint or pastel at all, finding that Flinders Blue Violet provided a richer, deeper colour. Sometimes the dark feathers were kissed by the mellow warmth of the sun and she'd use touches of yellow. The under belly feathers reflected various subtle shades of blues and pinks from the water. The pelican's neck was streaked with warm greys, and the bristly feathers at the crest were flecked with pure white. She loved capturing them in a variety of poses; cruising the shallows, spreading their wings, snapping their bills, preening their feathers, squatting on poles, or snoozing with their heads and long necks tucked away in the plumage.

Her mobile phone rang and she took it from the pocket of her jeans and frowned. She didn't recognise the number.

'Hi,' she said.

'Jaz. This is Doug.' There was a pause. 'Your dad.'

'Oh.' *Why was he calling? How did he get her number anyway?*

'I'm coming to the coast on business and I was hoping we could catch up.'

'Well, um,' Jasmine murmured.

'I've spoken to Susie. She's okay with it. Maybe we could meet at one of those little cafes near the beach. Susie doesn't really want me at the house.'

'Sure. Yeah. That would be okay. But I work most days.'

'Where are you working?'

'At the zoo. I do the photos. You know, take pictures of the tourists with the animals.'

'Good one. Well I'll call later to arrange a time and place. Bye.'

Jasmine grasped the phone and felt all the old emotions welling up inside. *Why turn up now? He was never interested before.* For a moment she was removed from this place, the sea, the pelicans, the peace. The air suddenly felt oppressive, it turned grey. It was if a curtain had fallen down and she was left exposed. They'd been a happy family once back in Sydney. Then he'd run off with that other chick. He messed up their world and threw them on the dump heap. She gritted her teeth. How could she forgive him, pretend none of that stuff ever happened?

She brushed a tear off her cheek and stood up. The sea breeze tiptoed across the park bringing with it the smells of anger and confusion. An old pelican wobbled towards her and she could see the bright yellow part of his eye as he tilted his head inquisitively.

'What are you looking at Mister?' she said, and she turned and walked towards the main road, her mind racing. *He turned our world upside down. Mum was never the same, and we had to struggle on. We had to leave Sydney, our friends, our schools, our home.*

The afternoon sun was throwing arrows of soft light through the pandanus trees and the traffic noises from the road echoed across the park as the workers returned to their homes at Pelican Waters. But Jasmine paid little attention.

She shared an old house with her mum and younger brother. It had been her grandparents' old cottage and it was a few blocks back from the beach. There were still a few of these old timber and fibro cottages scattered around Golden Beach. They were relics of the early days when Caloundra was a small fishing and beach community. Now the population had swelled, as more people discovered this popular holiday destination. There were now hundreds of holiday units, high-rise apartments and modern homes. The old fishing cottages were wedged between the concrete block modern homes which were often square-like and featureless hiding behind tall soldier fences.

She noticed her mum Susie's white Toyota parked in the driveway. She'd had the early day shift at the Retirement Home where she worked as a nurse's aide, and had just arrived home. The welcoming smell of coffee and baking greeted Jasmine as she walked in the door.

Susie turned from the sink. 'Hi Jaz. Have a good day off?'

'Yeah. Okay I guess.' Jasmine put her camera on the table and sat down, her chin on her hand. She watched her mum making coffee. Susie was still in her uniform, a blue shirt and black pants. Normally her dark hair was long and wavy, but she'd recently cut it very short in a boy style and it suited her fine features, high cheekbones and big brown eyes. She was shorter than Jasmine and small-boned, some might say angular. She had been going to the gym and it was paying off. She looked trim and toned although she still reckoned she had a big butt. Jasmine was watching her weight too. Her friend Amanda had huge weight problems, and she saw how it affected her;

poor self esteem, the relentless comments. She was determined not to get like that.

The kitchen was the family meeting place, it always felt safe and comfortable. Nothing much had changed since her grandfather had lived here. The same formica-topped table and vinyl chairs, the yellow canisters on top of the dresser, the lace cafe curtains gracing the window. She never knew her grandmother because she died before she was born. But she felt her presence here. Her grandfather talked so much about her that she figured she knew her pretty well. The photos showed a small lady with fine features, smiling warmly at the camera. She knew that Susie had been devastated by her mother's death. After all, she was still in her teens when it happened. No one wants to lose their mum so early. Maybe that's why Susie was often highly strung and so protective of her and Stephen.

Susie turned to face her daughter. 'Jaz tell me why I'm doing this job?' She sighed. 'Those old biddies at the Home nearly drive me crazy.'

'Oh Mum they can't be that bad. Just think of the bucks. That's why you do it. I wouldn't work either if I didn't have to.'

Susie sat down with the coffees. She pushed a plate of biscuits across the table. 'Here have one. Left over from morning tea.'

She sipped her coffee and looked at her daughter, fine auburn hair pulled back loosely in a ponytail, wayward strands brushing her face. Sometimes Jasmine looked so serious and withdrawn. She often wondered what was going on behind those deep set brown eyes of hers. Doug's eyes were like that; deep, impenetrable pools. Jasmine's moods were often like some of her paintings, seemingly easy to interpret but much more complex underneath. She seemed to be losing weight too and she couldn't afford to do that as she was already quite thin. But Susie dare not say anything or she'd risk getting her head bitten off. She wanted to protect her. God knows she'd been through enough with the family break up. And now bloody Doug would stir it all up again.

'Jaz did you get a call, from Doug?'

'Yeah. I don't know why the interest all of a sudden. What's it all about?'

'I'm not sure either. He called me and said he'd be up this way.' Susie sighed and looked away. 'Didn't really want to see me, only you and Stephen.'

Jasmine looked around. 'Where is Stephen? Home from school yet?'

'Not yet. He's gone to Mark's. Should be here soon.'

They turned to look as the screen door opened, and Stephen slouched in, his bag over his shoulder.

'Speak of the devil,' Susie said.

'Yeah right,' he mumbled and walked down the hall.

'Always a bag of laughs,' Jasmine smirked.

'Doug wants to see Stephen too. But I don't think that's going to happen,' Susie said.

'Well I don't want to go on my own,' Jasmine said.

'Stephen. Can you come here please? ' Susie called down the hallway. 'Now, not tomorrow.' She sighed.

He ambled in and leaned on the wall, his grey school shirt hanging out over his shorts which hung low over his hips. His unruly curls fell over his face and he brushed them aside roughly.

'Yeah.'

'Your dad called. He's coming to the coast on the weekend and he wants to see you and Jasmine. He wants to meet you for a coffee somewhere.'

'Jaz can go,' he mumbled. 'I don't want to see that prick. Ever.' And he whipped around and stormed off to his room.

Jasmine raised her eyebrows. 'No surprises there. I don't want to go either.'

'Well I don't blame either of you. But, look, he has a new business, marketing I think. He might offer to help you, financially I mean.'

'Mum. As if. Why would he want to help now? He never did before.'

'Well who knows? Anyway just think about it. You've got a few days to decide what to do.'

'What's for dinner Mum?'

'I'm making some pasta. You both like that.'

Jasmine scraped the chair back. 'I'm having a shower,' she said. Her phone beeped and she read the message from Amanda. She wanted to meet at the tavern for a drink at seven. Jasmine glanced at her watch. Time for a shower and a quick bite.

TWO

Brad's rough hands gripped the steering wheel and the ute spun in the gravel as he turned into the main road. *Stupid bitch. Who did she think she was anyhow?* Normally he would have dumped the rubbish, but his mind was a million miles away. Everyone was on his case lately. He wished they'd all just give him a break. He had more to worry about than a stupid plastic bag. But she was a nice looking chick. What was he thinking? He could have chatted her up instead of getting aggro.

He exited the roundabout and joined the Nicklin Way. Northbound traffic was building up as workers headed home, the soft mellow light of the sunset painting the landscape with brush strokes of gold and soft pinks.

Fishing gave Brad the escape he so badly needed, escape from the monotony and isolation of work on the trawling boat, and refuge from the troubles of his old man. He never knew what to expect next. His father was an angry man with issues, the conflicts of a tormented war veteran.

He pulled into the driveway of his parents' house at Mooloolaba, a modest low set timber house with a small, sad backyard. A broken concrete path led to the front stairs where three steps crawled up to the small patio, a couple of outdoor chairs dozing in the corner. His mother had tried to make the little outdoor area more inviting by putting out some pot plants, but even these looked a bit tired. This place was about all they could afford now his dad was on a pension. Even when he was in work they never had much, so Brad liked to help out when he could.

He grabbed a couple of fish fillets out of the esky, and went up the stairs. His mum Cheryl was watching a game show on TV. He could hear the contestant saying, 'Case number 10 thanks.' Cheryl jumped up as he entered.

'Brad Love. How are you?' She moved over to hug him but he stepped back.

'No Mum. I'm smelly as. I'll just put the fish in the fridge. I've gotta go.' He grabbed some cling wrap, folded it around the fillets and put them in the freezer. He turned to go but Cheryl grabbed his sleeve.

'Won't you stay for a coffee? I could cook the fish for all of us.' A car horn blared out the front and a dark, stooped figure emerged from the hallway. Brad's father John shuffled past, nodded at Brad, grunted under his breath and stumbled off to the waiting car.

'Off to the RSL,' Cheryl said as she watched her husband's departing figure.

'How is he anyway?'

'You know your father. Nothing's changed.' Then she quickly said, 'When do you go out again?'

'I've got a couple more days off. But there's a cyclone sitting off the coast. It could mess things up a bit.'

As Brad walked off, Cheryl held the screen door. Brad was her only son, a solid build like his father and dark curly hair. He was deeply tanned, and she thought, very healthy looking. At least she got that part right, providing healthy food for her family. Whenever he had the chance he was off fishing, and he would bring her some of his catch. Because he worked in that rough sea environment he often went unshaven and it gave him a menacing look. But she knew her Brad. He could be a real softie. That dimpled smile of his would always win her over. She sighed and her body slumped against the door frame. *John's gone off with his Vietnam mates and Brad has his own life. I don't really feel like eating fish on my own.*

She relied a lot on Brad for moral support. It was a lonely life with a tormented man in the house. She was scared to go out with him because his unpredictable behaviour would draw unwanted attention. She had a few women friends and colleagues at the Surf Club where she worked and she had coffee with them occasionally, or they would see a movie. But she dare not invite them to her morbid place.

She let the door swing back on its catch and returned to the TV show to see how much money was now on offer.

Brad often wondered what the future held for her. He might not be around forever and then where would she turn? She had to start thinking about herself and treat herself every now and then, instead of being dictated to by the old man's needs and demands. But he couldn't force her. She'd have to do it herself.

He stopped at the bottle shop on the way home. He knew there'd be no booze left in the fridge. That prick Andy always pinched his piss. Said he'd pay him back but he never did.

The flat was in a tree-lined street a few blocks from Mooloolaba beach. It was a neglected timber building, an old house that had been divided into two flats, one up, one down. The developers hadn't grabbed it yet, but it was only a matter of time. The land was too valuable. Mooloolaba was now a bustling centre of high rise apartments poking up like tombstones, stop-start traffic, busy cafes and alfresco restaurants, bars, shops and nightclubs. A great place to live, but the down side were all the freeloaders wanting somewhere to crash.

He packed away his fishing gear and lumbered up the small set of splintered steps with the esky. The place smelt of dirty dishes and mull. Andy was lying back on the sofa, his head in a cloud of smoke.

'Hey Dude,' he said, propping himself up on one elbow. 'More supplies.'

'Nope. Think again mate. These are mine.' Brad ripped the lid off one and had a swig, then put the others in the fridge.

'Hey that chick Julia called. Said your phone must be off or something. Wants you to call her,' Andy said. He took another drag, inhaling deeply.

Brad frowned. He'd call her later but he needed to charge his phone first, have a few beers and relax. She could wait. He'd only known her a few months and she was a nice chick really. Good looking, a great body. She didn't like him being away on the trawler so much. 'It's a dangerous job and you're never home. Can't you find something else?' she'd said. But Brad loved the sea. It was a wild feeling out there, the wind ripping your face and hair, the way you braced your body against the monotonous pitch and roll of the vessel, the taste and rawness of it. And it was tough work. Not for the weak or faint-hearted, wrestling trawling nets, hauling wet, knotted ropes, heaving bulky crates. Skin turned to leather and hands and feet cracked and bled.

He flopped into one of the tattered lounge chairs, and took another gulp of beer. He flicked the television on. A bald middle-aged man was leaping around, hugging the compere of a game show. Golden snowflakes were showering down on them from the ceiling. The beaming contestant waved a huge faux cheque in the air. He'd just won $ 50,000.

Julia called around just as Brad stepped out on his way to get some takeaway.

'Didn't Andy give you my message?' she asked, her hands on her hips.

'I just got home. My phone's out of charge. I was going to call you,' he said, swinging the door of the ute open.

'Hang on. Hang on. Where are you going?' She grabbed his arm.

'I want some takeaway. I'm bloody starving.'

'Wait, I'll drive. We'll go to the pub and get something there. I need to talk.'

What now? Always bloody talk. Some women! ... But you never know I might get lucky later.

'Better change out of your fishing clothes. You smell,' she said as she screwed her face up.

The pub was noisy as usual, but not crowded as this was a Monday. The population seemed to swell twofold on weekends, even more during holidays. There were scattered groups of people drinking and eating, trying to make conversation over the top of Lady Gaga. They ordered their meals and found a table on the veranda. A cool breeze came in from the ocean, the crash of the waves competing with the pub noise.

'Brad,' Julia said. 'I've something to tell you.'

Here goes. Another bloody lecture. She doesn't give up. He sighed and swallowed some beer. She sipped on her juice.

'I'm going away. To Sydney.' She paused and twirled the straw in her drink. 'My nan's sick and I've decided to go and live there for a while, get a job.'

'What? When?'

'Tomorrow. I leave tomorrow.'

'What about us? I thought we were doing alright together.'

'Well we aren't really suited. Besides, I never see you. You're always out at sea. What sort of relationship is that?' She dropped her head and wiped her nose. Brad rubbed his hand through his hair.

'So I suppose that's it then,' he mumbled. The meals arrived and Julia sniffed into a tissue. They ate in their own silence enveloped in the unfeeling ambience of the pub.

Brad was confused. Part of him wanted Julia to stay, she was good company and he loved the sex. But she'd been very possessive and always telling him what he should do and he hated that. Everyone was on his back and he'd had enough. Taking a break was probably a good thing in a way. He had eaten his steak and chips quickly but Julia was still fussing with her salad. He pushed the chair back.

'I need to hang a leak. Do you want another drink?'

'No. I'm right,' Julia mumbled.

After using the bathroom he leant on the bar and scanned the room. A slim girl with wavy shoulder length auburn hair got up from a table she was sharing with another girl, straightened her jeans and flicked her hair back. He recognised that face, the fine features, the deep set eyes. *Of course, the boat ramp. The pelican girl.*

'Well hello again,' he grinned as she approached. Her mouth fell open a little and she frowned.

'Pelican Girl. Remember. You told me off for leaving rubbish,' he said. She stopped then her face clouded.

'Yeah. Well you deserved it.'

'Don't be too hard on me. I'm really a nice guy.' He took his drink. 'See ya round,' he said raising his glass.

When he got back to the table, Julia was rummaging in her bag. He noticed that her eyes were red and he felt at a loss. What could he say?

'Hurry up with that drink,' she said. 'I want to go.'

'I'm sorry, I don't want you to go but it's probably for the best. Have a break.'

She glared at him. 'I don't think you'll miss me too much. It didn't take you long to hit onto another chick,' she said looking over to where the girl's table was.

'Hang on a minute. That was a stupid bird who told me off today at the boat ramp. She pissed me off.'

'Yeah, well you didn't look too pissed off to me. Let's go.'

When they pulled up at the flat, Brad reached out to her. But she brushed him off. 'I might call when I'm settled. Bye Brad.'

He stood on the street until her little white Datsun had turned the corner.

THREE

The weather had turned foul yesterday and Jasmine had gone to bed listening to the incessant rain and the whistling wind which raged through the night. Did her mum just call? The room was dim and cosy. *Too early to get up.* She squinted at the digital bedside clock.

Yep. 7am. Wednesday. She yawned and turned over willing the clock to be wrong.

'Jaz, Jaz.'

'Coming,' she called.

'Jaz, come and see this.' This time it sounded urgent. Jasmine shuffled down the hall running her hand through her tangled hair.

'Look,' her mum pointed to the TV. It was the morning news program. The images were of a huge container ship and an ocean streaked with oil. Jasmine moved closer not understanding the urgency until she heard the newsreader. A cargo ship had lost some of its containers in the wild weather and the ship's hull had been damaged, sending tonnes of oil leaking into the ocean.

'God what a mess. Where is it?' Jasmine sat on the edge of the lounge chair.

'Here, off Moreton Island. So far it's east of the island, but they are worried the currents will bring it further north...onto our beaches.'

'What about the poor birds? And all the other wildlife?' Jasmine said. She'd seen images of birds trying to clean their oil-covered feathers and then ingesting the vile stuff. She couldn't begin to imagine blobs of the foul smelling oil polluting the beaches. She wondered what the government agencies were going to do and knew they'd have to act fast or this could be a major disaster.

At work that day, the oil spill was the main topic of conversation. It turned out that the containers that toppled overboard were full of ammonium nitrate, another chemical hazard that would have to be dealt with. Some of the tourists said they'd be packing up and heading home if the oil reached the beaches where they were holidaying. Jasmine shuddered at the thought of what it would do to the coast's environment, animals and tourist industry. How could this happen? Why was the ship out in such rough weather? Why didn't they secure the containers properly? She'd heard that the ship was now docked in Brisbane and not permitted to leave until the situation had been fully investigated.

Within days the oil monster had deposited its putrid ooze on a 60 kilometre stretch of coastline, covering beaches, rocky reefs, and coastal and mangrove wetlands as far north as Marcoola. The government had declared it a disaster zone and gathered agencies and volunteers to help clean up.

At the end of the week Jasmine joined some of her work colleagues, donning orange overalls and gloves, moving slowly up the northern beaches of Bribie painstakingly removing the toxic mess. The beaches had already been hammered by Cyclone Hamish and there was a lot of debris and steeply eroded sand banks.

'I hope they hit that shipping line with a massive fine,' Jasmine's friend Amanda said. She looked like the Michelin man in her oversized orange suit. Jasmine smiled at the image.

'Look at us,' Jasmine said. 'We look like astronauts or something. Not exactly the most flattering of suits.' They both laughed as they hauled their rubbish bags to the pick-up vehicle, and added theirs to the moaning pile.

'Hey Jaz, isn't that the guy you saw at the pub the other night?' Amanda was looking at a strong young man also in overalls helping people load bags into the next truck. Just then he looked over and smiled. He started walking over, and Jasmine shrank and moved behind Amanda's bulk.

'Oh no. Let's move.'

'Too late,' Amanda whispered. She straightened up and smiled.

'Hi, I'm Amanda and you are...'

'Brad.'

'This is Jasmine... or Jaz,' she said moving aside. 'But I think you have already met.'

'Yep. We have kind of,' he said. Jasmine looked up and half smiled. She couldn't help it. He actually looked okay now he'd shaved, and when he smiled she noticed a dimple in his cheek, kinda cute she thought. He took his hat off and tossed his head.

'Pretty hot work. You girls got some water?'

'Yeah. We're fine,' Amanda said, and turned, but Jasmine had already walked off.

'Hey you could have stayed a bit,' Amanda said jogging clumsily to catch up. 'He seems really nice.'

'Yeah. Seems nice. Just rubs me up the wrong way.'

'Well I think he's hot. You need a guy like him. I'd chat him up if I wasn't already hitched.'

The two girls continued up the beach to where they'd been working. They squatted and started prizing away bits of the oily gunk with their trowels. It was tedious work, and with 100 workers on this kilometre stretch of beach alone, it was clear the clean up was going to take some time.

'How are the wedding plans going?' Jasmine asked.

'Don't ask. Dave's keeping out of it and I don't blame him. I didn't think that a wedding could be so much hassle. I now know why some couples go to a secluded island somewhere to get married.'

'Why don't you?'

'That wouldn't work. Dave's an only child and his family expect a big do. His mum and dad want this huge thing, but my parents are struggling. They can't afford anything that big.'

'Can't they let Dave's parents pay if they're well off and that's what they want?'

Amanda shook her head. 'My parents wouldn't feel right. They'd want to pay their way. I'm afraid they're going to go into debt and then how would I feel?'

'Well maybe you'll just have to talk to Dave's oldies. Tell them to tone it down a bit.'

'Yeah I guess.' Amanda wiped the back of her gloved hand across her brow. 'God it's so hot. I think I'd rather be back serving burgers in the cafe. This is shit.' She flopped back in the sand and stretched her legs. Her face was red and she seemed as if she would burst out of the suit any minute.

Jasmine often dreamed of her own wedding, although hers would be a little simpler than Amanda's. Not for her the crowd of people and the flashy dress. She would wear a Hollywood style gown. She imagined herself like Nicole Kidman in the Chanel ad. The wedding would be at the beach, the gentle wind blowing her hair and veil. She would lift the delicate fabric of her gown, and the gentle waves would whisper and ebb around her bare feet. Amanda's voice broke her reverie.

'Hey have you caught up with your father yet?'

Jasmine had filled her in on the phone calls, and her reluctance to meet up with the man who'd deserted them all those years ago.

'Tomorrow at the Silvio's Cafe. I probably won't even recognise him. It's been about eleven or so years.'

'He's probably the same. You're the one who's changed. You were what, about ten?'

'Yeah I was in about year five and Stephen was just starting kindergarten. It was a shock for us kids because we thought everything was okay. Mum kept her feelings to herself. Well I suppose you would with such young kids. It was so hard. We couldn't understand why he didn't want us anymore.'

'That must have been awful. But at least you had your mum. And she's so nice.'

When Jasmine arrived at the cafe on Saturday morning she scanned the tables. It wasn't too busy yet. Doug was seated in a far corner reading the paper. She noticed he was wearing reading glasses, hadn't needed those before. Jasmine paused and swallowed hard. Her dad did look much the same, smart and suave, clean-shaven, a crisp business shirt. She remembered how he spent a lot of time on grooming. Always made sure he was well dressed, and his hands were always soft and immaculate, even the nails manicured. She moved forward weaving between the tables. He looked over his glasses and jumped up nearly knocking the condiment and menu holder flying.

'Jaz. Look at my girl.' He wrapped his arms around her. He smelled of spice aftershave. He stepped back and held her hands. 'You look great,' he said. Jasmine felt weird. What do you say? This man, her dad, was really a stranger.

'Here sit,' he said pulling out a chair. 'I'll get us some coffee. Do you want something to eat?'

Jasmine shook her head. 'No. I'm fine thanks.' She watched him walk away. *He married Mum, had us kids. It all seemed okay back then. What went wrong? How could he just wipe us like that?*

They sat in an awkward space as they sipped their coffees. Jasmine kept her head down, scooping the froth and licking her spoon. She could feel his eyes on her.

'Do you like your zoo job?'

'It's okay.' She looked out over the esplanade to the Passage. her eyes following the kite surfers as they dipped and jumped over the waves, their colourful chutes billowing out.

'You know Jaz you can do better than that.'

She turned to face him. 'What do you mean?'

'The zoo job. You can do better than that. You're too smart. You should be studying. Aim higher.'

Jasmine glared at him. 'What would you know?' she said bitterly. 'You weren't there. You wouldn't know how I went in school. You--'

'Hang on a minute. I just feel you're wasting your time taking photos. Have you thought of something more long term?'

Jasmine shrugged. 'Get real. I don't have the money for uni and Mum can't afford it. You know that.' She sipped her coffee and watched a young couple walking past pushing a stroller.

'Well I could help.'

Jasmine stared at him. 'Why now? Where were you when we really needed the help?' She seethed. Her eyes smarted and suddenly the coffee taste in her mouth turned sour. She pushed the chair back.

'Jaz, Stop. I know all that. Please.' He grabbed her arm as she started to go. 'I want to be part of your life...and Stephen's. It's not too late.'

By now Jasmine was aware that several patrons were glancing in their direction. 'Thanks for the coffee,' she said and she marched off, tears smearing her face. *You can't just start being a father when it suits you. What a prick!*

FOUR

The winches screeched as the trawler's booms were slowly raised and the "Susan Marie" eased her way into Mooloolaba Harbour. Up in the wheel house Brad watched the early morning joggers and walkers enjoying the many paths bordering the canal. An osprey perched high in the dead limbs of a tea tree surveyed the scene like a lord looking over his kingdom. Jacko and Nick were down below getting the crates ready for when they docked at the Fisheries. It had been a short trip this time. Things were looking grim and Jacko had been in a perpetual bad mood. There was all the rough weather last week and now the oil spill had put a huge question mark over all fishing activities in the area. Who knows how the oily muck affected the fish and prawns? Jacko had a missus, two kids and a mortgage. He'd be battling for a while if this oil thing messed things up. And Brad knew he and Nick would be back on the dole.

When they'd finished unpacking and cleaning up, Nick drove Brad back to the flat. Brad went inside, dropped his bag and grabbed his ute keys. He was starving and he knew the cupboard and fridge would be yawning at him, so he drove to the small shopping village not far from the flat and bought some bread, milk and cereal.

His mind was a million miles away as he drove away from the shops. He yawned and rubbed his facial stubble which was rough and salt-encrusted. His eyes felt dry and itchy and he stank like fish. *Can't wait for a bloody good shower, some decent tucker and then some shut-eye.*

Suddenly he hit the brakes as he saw the speed radar gun. *Too late. Fuck. The bastards got me.* The patrol officer stepped out and waved him to the kerb. Brad pulled up and banged his head on his hand. *Shit, shit. Bloody cops. I wasn't going that fast. I can't afford a fine. Shit, shit.*

He arrived back at the flat still swearing. The place was disorganised and messy as usual, but he didn't have the energy or the motivation to bother with tidying up now. That prick Andy should clean up his own mess. He stood under the shower washing away days of salt and hard work. After a huge helping of cereal he crashed out, his body still rolling on the ocean waves.

Through the fuzzy curtain of sleep Brad heard his phone go off. He rolled over and dozed. The bloody thing kept ringing. He grabbed it and looked at the screen. Mum.

'Yeah Mum. What's up?'

'Brad can you come over? Your father's had a fall.'

Brad propped himself up, squinted and looked at his watch. Four pm. Could he have slept that long?

'What? Where?'

'He was out at the club. The bus dropped him off. He's pissed. He's at the bottom of the stairs and I can't move him.'

Leave the old fart there. He can rot for all I care.

'Okay. Okay. I'll get over as soon as I can.'

Later Brad pulled up in the driveway and straightaway noticed the lump of clothing slumped at the end of the path. Cheryl was hovering at the top of the stairs. She stepped over the lifeless shape and pulled one arm while Brad grabbed the other.

'Come on Dad. Get up. You can't stay here.' His father struggled to move, then looked at Brad with red, bleary eyes.

'Whad would you know... anyow... no fuckn idea,' his father slurred, saliva dribbling onto his grubby shirt. He high-stepped and moaned. They managed to lift and slide his dead weight across the patio then inside onto the sofa.

'Bwad, you. Bloody useless.' He fell back, closed his eyes and started snoring.

'Don't worry about him. He doesn't know what he's saying,' Cheryl said. 'Come and have a cup of tea.' Brad was used to the put-downs, but it still hurt even now that he was older. He could never be good enough for his father. How could you work it out? Was it jealousy? His father's own inadequacy? He only stayed around because of his mum, because she needed some support.

'Mum you know this can't keep up. It'll drive you crazy. How can you live with someone like this?' Cheryl put the kettle on, slumped into a chair and lit up a cigarette.

'I don't know what to do. He's getting worse.' She took a long drag and exhaled. 'He has nightmares. Screams out at night. He's so angry and bitter.'

'He doesn't hit you does he?'

His mother looked down and straightened her skirt. 'No... no. But he's changed. He's losing his mind. He imagines things. He hears helicopters and gunfire. Brad I'm scared.' She started to cry. Brad sighed. This was not the first time this had happened. He was at a loss.

'Well you'll have to get help. A psycho or someone. Anyway Mum I have to go.' *I can't handle this. Jesus Christ I've had enough of all this shit.* He often felt like he was shackled to her and the situation. Something had to give.

Andy arrived at the flat just as Brad returned from the family dramas.

'Guess what man. I've got me a job,' Andy said.

'Great,' Brad said with a hint of sarcasm.

'Yep. You're looking at the new snake handler.'

'You're fucking kidding aren't you?' Brad scoffed. 'You can handle only one snake I know of.' And he smiled as he grabbed a beer from the fridge. Andy was following him like an excited pup.

'Ask me. Go on.'

'Give me a break would ya.' Brad's humour had quickly subsided as he pushed past his flatmate.

'It's at the zoo, man. Can you believe it?' Andy said. Brad took a mouthful of ale and burped.

'How the fuck could you get a job like that? You're always high. You won't last a day.'

'Yes I will. Wait and see. I worked out bush with my uncle. I know a lot about snakes.'

'You're so full of shit,' Brad said.

'And you should see the chicks who work there Brad. I'll be in heaven mate.'

Brad shook his head and turned the television on.

It was Tuesday and it would be another busy day at the zoo. The front car park was already full and four huge tourist buses had spilled out loads of eager tourists. A noisy mob of school children flowed towards the stadium in readiness for the Bird Show. Jasmine picked up her camera ready for the 11 o'clock photo session. Several groups of excited tourists had already lined up, eager for their chance to hold a koala. This would be the first time many of them had seen or held a koala. A small girl with the first group kept pestering her grandparents. 'Where is it? Where is the koala?' She was restless, swinging under the queue ropes, and jumping up and down on the photo platform. Her grandma kept pulling her back. 'Wait here Chloe. The koala will be here soon,' her grandma said. Just then Megan, one of the assistants, came out with Jacob, the koala for this session. The staff at the zoo made sure they rotated the koalas for this duty as they became stressed with all the handling. The little girl's bravado changed and she clung to her grandma's skirt, refusing to hold the koala. She snuggled into her grandpa as grandma held Jacob. No amount of coaxing would bring a smile for the camera. Jasmine found it interesting dealing with the melting pot of people; young ones, old people, visitors from a variety of countries. It was different every day.

She had almost finished the koala groups when she noticed Brian bringing out Bertha the Burmese Python for the snake photos. Jasmine was not particularly fond of snakes, but she was not scared. She couldn't understand why some people wanted to be photographed with one, and one as huge as Bertha. It took two men to carry Bertha. Jasmine's eyes were drawn to the new guy with Brian. She hadn't seen him around before. He was tall and athletic-looking with sandy hair, a bit like Brett Lee the cricketer, she thought. She must have been staring because she jumped when Megan spoke.

'He's kinda cute hey?'

'Who, the python?' Jasmine joked. Megan winked at her then walked away taking Jacob back to his enclosure. There were only two groups waiting for snake photos, so Jasmine was able to chat to the boys. Brian introduced them and Jasmine smiled widely. When Andy spoke she was mesmerised. She'd never felt like this before. The guy sure had charisma. He turned as he and Brian shuffled off with Bertha.

'See you for lunch,' he said as he put on a funny walk.

'He's a quick one,' Megan said. 'Watch him.'

At lunchtime Jasmine walked over to the Reptile House and stood outside Bertha's cage. She couldn't see Andy around. She started reading the information board. "The Burmese Pythons are among the largest snakes in the world. They are native to South-East Asia. They can grow up to seven metres in length and can weigh up to 90 kilograms." *That's some snake.*

She jumped as a hand touched her shoulder.

'Interesting hey?' Andy said.

'I can't believe their size,' Jasmine said. 'My aunty went to Malaysia a few years ago and brought back a newspaper clipping showing a photo of a python that had eaten a goat! Can you imagine that? How would it get its chops around a goat?' They both laughed as Jasmine shivered and grimaced.

They walked off to the cafe and bought drinks and salad rolls. Andy bought a bucket of hot chips as well. 'I'm starving,' he said as Jasmine shook her head.

'How long have you worked here?' he asked as they unwrapped their rolls.

'About a year. What about you?'

He spread his arms wide. 'Can't you tell? First day.'

Jasmine smiled and wiped her mouth. 'Wow you've slotted in well.'

'Yeah. I'm only part-time yet, but I think I really like this place. As long as I don't have to pick up elephant poo or help the camels give birth.' His blue eyes came alive, deep pools that sucked you in.

'Well someone's gotta do it,' Jasmine said screwing her nose. She sipped on her iced coffee. 'So where do you live Andy... or is it Andrew?'

'I've been called many names but Andy's fine. I'm at Mooloolaba, great spot. And I was born here on the coast not a blow-in like many others.'

'Excuse me. I'm one of those so called Southerners.'

'Oops. Sorry...So where do you call home?'

'Right now I'm living with my mum and daggy fifteen year old brother at Golden Beach.' She rolled her eyes. 'Yes uncool Golden Beach... but I get out occasionally. My friends and I often come to Mooloolaba for some action.'

'How about dinner one night? Can I meet you at the tavern? ' he said.

'Sure. That'd be good.' Andy offered to pick her up but Jasmine said she had her own car. She didn't want to appear too eager. She'd only just met the guy. But she loved his charm, his humour. She felt happy around him and that was good wasn't it?

FIVE

Meeting her dad at the cafe had been a big mistake. Jasmine thought she was doing the right thing. How could she have gotten it so wrong? It only opened old wounds, ones she'd thought had healed or been covered up long ago.

'You should have accepted his help,' Susie said later. 'You could do the uni course you've always wanted to do. You could work in the Animal Hospital. You'd love that.'

'Mum. I don't want his money. I want to make my own way. What does he want out of it anyway? Glory? To lessen his guilt? Come on. It's always been about him.'

'Well I wouldn't be knocking it back. It's about time he offered support.'

Jasmine felt hollow inside. She was light-headed, faint. 'I'm going for a walk. I need some air,' she said.

'What about your dinner?' Susie said.

'I'm not hungry,' Jasmine mumbled as she strode out the front door. Susie followed her.

'Jaz. Don't go far in the dark,' she called. Her voice echoed off the street.

Susie went back inside and dished up the meal. She put Jasmine's dinner in the microwave, although she knew she probably wouldn't eat it. Her daughter seemed to eat less and less lately. She was looking pale and gaunt too. Stephen said he heard her throwing up in the toilet. What was going on with her? She'd read somewhere that this behaviour was caused by emotional problems. If it continued she'd take her to a doctor. She didn't want an anorexic daughter.

'Stephen. Dinner,' she called. She took her plate of food into the lounge and sat down. The local news program had just started on TV. There were more images of the oil spill. "The 30 containers of ammonium nitrate that fell off the Pacific Adventurer on Wednesday morning remain a major concern to commercial fishermen," the newsreader said. He continued, "A spokesman for the Seafood Industry said that the containers are located right in the middle of the major trawl grounds." Susie stopped eating and frowned. *So it's not just the oil. It's these other toxins too. What a disaster.*

'Stephen,' she called again. He sauntered out, picked up his plate and headed down the hall.

'I'll eat in here. I've got assignments to do,' he said. She heard the bedroom door close. She looked down at the plate. The food was starting to taste like glue. Her throat ached and the tears started to well up. *Is this all there is? Work everyday? Left on my own with two kids with problems I can't fix? Bills and more bills? I've had enough.*

She got up, threw her plate in the sink, then locked herself in the shower. Tears flowed freely as she stepped under the warm stream.

It was velvety dark as Jasmine sat on the rocks at the edge of the Passage, her long Indian-style skirt wrapped around her legs. Some yellow light came from the street lamp above the boat ramp about fifty metres away to the north. To the south she could see the blue navigation light on the bridge to Pelican Waters, and the Jetty apartment lights danced on the ripples. She took deep breaths of the fresh, salty air. The pelicans had gone off to their roosting spots, but she could hear the chorus of the noisy terns on the sandbanks. There must have been hundreds of them out there.

She looked towards the ramp as she heard a car pull up. It was a white, late model car. It seemed that no one was getting out. She was not afraid because they wouldn't be able to see her on such a dark night. Not long after, another car pulled in beside the first one. It was much older, with a rough, coughing engine. The drivers of both vehicles got out. They were both men, one tall and thin and he was wearing a baseball cap, and the other man older and shorter, but he was smartly dressed in business clothes. There was muffled conversation and parcels were exchanged. Jasmine crept forward, taking cover behind the cotton trees and low shrubs. She caught snatches of words. Something about this Friday night. *What's going on?* She shivered. The noisy car took off, but the older man started walking in her direction. *Shit.* She could smell familiar aftershave so he must have been very close. She crouched down in the bushes and realised he was having a piss. She peered out as he walked back to the car, doing up his fly and adjusting his pants. He turned and looked out at the water, his face partially visible under the street lamp. Jasmine's hand flew to her mouth. *Dad. Could it be Dad? What's he doing out here? I thought he was back in Sydney.*

He slipped behind the wheel and drove off slowly, slowly enough for Jasmine to see the luminescent sticker on the back. "Sunshine Rentals".

Jasmine waited until she was sure neither car was coming back, and she headed home via the boat ramp street. Something on the bitumen surface near where the cars had been parked caught her eye. *Not another plastic bag.* She picked it up expecting a broken, gooey bag, but it was new and sealed. She held it up to the light. Then she went cold. *White powder. Shit. It couldn't be. Those guys must have dropped it. Chuck it in the bin Jaz.* She did have a vivid imagination at times, but this, this could be drugs, cocaine or something. *If I'm found with it, God knows what will happen. But then if those guys are involved with this stuff it needs to be reported.* She'd do the right thing. Take it to the cops. But that's all. No other information. She didn't see anyone. Leave it at that. Maybe she could call her father to see if he was back in Sydney, then she'd know it wasn't him after all. No. She had a better idea.

'Good Evening, Sunshine Rentals,' the girl answered cheerily.

'Oh hi,' Jasmine said. 'I was wondering if you could help me. I'm trying to contact my father who's up here from Sydney. His mobile seems to be turned off or out of charge. I met up with him the other day and I know he was hiring a car from you. I'm wondering what address he's given?'

'What name was it?'

'Bennett...Doug Bennett.' Jasmine could hear the computer keys clicking.

'Let's see...Bennett. He's staying at the Hyatt.'

'Thanks. I hope I haven't missed him. How long did he book the car for?' Jasmine asked.

'He's got it for another week,' the girl said. Jasmine thanked her, pocketing her mobile and the small plastic bag.

Her mind was racing. Where to now? Just because he hired the car didn't necessarily mean it was him at the boat ramp. And even if it was him, it could have been quite innocent, just two friends meeting. She decided to wait and see what the lab test on the plastic bag revealed. And she would check out the Friday night meeting they mentioned.

The next morning she dropped the bag off at the local police station. She was glad to be rid of it. Of course she had to give all the details; time, place, and her own movements. The older police officer at the front desk said he wasn't sure what it was, but they would have it tested. He said he would contact her about the result and then, if it was drugs, she'd need to come in for elimination printing. She didn't tell Susie. It would be best to keep this quiet for a while. Besides it could all be nothing.

It was Wednesday evening and Jasmine was excited about her date with Andy. She'd fussed with her lip liner and lipstick but her lips still looked shapeless. *Why was I born with lips like these? Maybe I should try botox.* She smacked her lips together and looked in the long mirror by her door, smoothing her hands over her upper body. *And my flat chest. I never look good in clothes with these small boobs.* She'd been teased at school for being flat as a board. She pushed her bra up and adjusted the straps. The gel inserts helped push up what little she had. She sighed and pulled on her white top. One last toss of her hair and she was off.

Andy was already at the bar when she arrived. He looked even more gorgeous out of his zoo uniform. *How could I be so lucky? What a hot guy.*

Andy turned as Jasmine approached. She looked like a model with her trim figure and fine features. The figure-hugging jeans clung to her long legs and her small perky breasts pushed at the plunging white top. *Cool.*

He stood and kissed her cheek and they sat at the bar enjoying their drinks and listening to the live music. Jasmine stuck to one vodka mix as she was driving. She couldn't afford to get caught. Then where would she be? She'd lose her job for sure. Andy made her laugh with his silly antics and the colour he added to the conversation. After dinner he held her hand and they walked to her little green Honda which was parked under the building. He stopped to answer a text then jumped in beside her.

When they pulled up at Andy's flat, he invited her in. 'Just a quick coffee,' Jasmine said. She wasn't going to rush with this one. She did that last time and her heart got ripped apart. Not again.

'Which one is yours?'Jasmine said as they passed the two vehicles in the driveway.

'This one of course,' Andy said as he tapped the bonnet of the new black ute. 'Do you like it?'

Jasmine was not sure what to say.

'Just kidding,' Andy said. 'It's Brad's. He makes more money than me. But soon...soon...'

Jasmine looked over at the bomb car beside it. It looked familiar. Andy's phone rang and he walked out near the road to answer it. Before she could comment on the call or the old car, Andy grabbed her arm and escorted her through the door into the flat. In the darkness, he bent and kissed her softly on the lips. It was warm and sensuous, and Jasmine melted into his arms. He smelt clean, manly, but there was hint of something else and she could smell it in the room. She pulled back and flicked on the light switch near the door.

'Do you smoke pot? I can smell it,' she said.

'Yeah. Brad and I have a bit every now and then. You must have tried it?'

'Once. I tried it once. I didn't want to go there,' Jasmine said. She looked around while Andy made the coffee. It was a typical boys' flat. The sink was stacked with dirty dishes and the rubbish bin was overflowing with old pizza boxes. Empty beer cans stood to attention on the coffee table. Someone had lined them up in an orderly row.

'What's your flatmate like?'

'Brad. He's okay. We go way back. We went to school together. He works on a trawler and they've been stuck at the wharf. Can't go out because of the oil spill problem. That makes him pretty aggro.'

Jasmine had a thought. *The black ute. Fishing.* 'Hey does he go fishing...you know apart from work? Does he have a tinnie?'

'Does a bear shit in the woods? He's a mad keen fisherman. He drinks and fishes. That's it, man.'

'I think I've met him. Quite solid and strong looking, curly dark hair.'

'That's the one. Where did you meet him?'

'I've seen him a couple of times. He has quite an attitude.'

Andy brought the coffees over and sat down. 'Brad's girl took off to Sydney so that made him mad. Then this problem with work. To top it all, his old man has mental problems.'

Andy put his arm around her and they settled back into the folds of the sofa.

'But enough talk of Brad,' Andy said. 'We've got better things to do.'

SIX

Mrs Jensen struggled to prop herself up as Susie tucked in the sheets at the bottom of the bed.

'Are you off now Susie?' she wheezed.

'Sure am Mrs Jensen. Can't wait to get home and put my feet up.'

'Don't forget to tell Ernie to come, will you?'

'I'll do that, Mrs Jensen. Now put your head back and have a rest,' Susie said as she fluffed the pillow and eased the old lady's head back. This is what Mrs Jensen asked every day, always wanting her dead husband. She was nearly ninety, and like many of the patients had Alzheimer's Disease. It was so sad. Susie hoped she never got that bad. How sad to lose your memory, not recognise your loved ones, become a shell of your former self. In earlier times, some of the old people tried to leave the home, they would wander all over the place, so now the facility was like a fortress with security gates.

As she drove home her thoughts went to Doug's phone call. He wanted to come over, have a chat. She was not so sure, but it couldn't hurt could it? She thought he'd gone back but he said he hadn't finished his business meetings yet. Sure she was devastated when he left her and the kids, but she'd never really stopped loving him. She never told the kids that. They'd been really hurt, wanted nothing to do with him. Maybe it was true what he said that he'd changed. He wasn't with Cindy anymore, in fact he said he was thinking of moving up here to the coast. She arranged to meet him tomorrow evening when she knew the kids weren't home. Stephen would be at soccer practice and Jasmine was helping Amanda choose wedding flowers.

She had just slipped out of her shoes and was putting the milk in the fridge when there was a knock at the door. There were two policemen standing there, an older officer and beside him a stocky, but attractive young female constable. They introduced themselves. Susie went cold. Police at the door. That was not a good thing.

Before she could panic further the officer said, 'It's nothing serious. We just want to talk to Jasmine Bennett. Is she home?'

'No she's not. She's not in any trouble is she?'

The man shook his head. 'No. No. We just need to talk to her. Can you tell her we called? She can ring me on this number.' He handed her a card. They walked back to their car and Susie stared at the card. What was going on? It wasn't like Jasmine to be in trouble.

Jasmine finished work early on that Thursday so she went to the park near the boat ramp. She'd managed to get some good action shots of the pelicans. A few fishing boats had come in and the birds gathered in their usual spot on the curve of beach near the filleting table. She picked her way over the rocks leading down to the sand, and then she saw fishing line hanging out of one old pelican's bill. She walked carefully towards him, but he kept moving into the huddle of birds. She could see that the line was tangled as it drooped to the ground, and it still had a sinker attached to it.

'Come on old boy, let me have a look,' she said. But he wouldn't let her get closer. She thought he probably swallowed the hook and it was stuck somewhere. She was worried about the tangled bits catching and injuring his legs. She decided to call the Bird Rescue Service in the hinterland. She'd seen it advertised at the zoo. They'd know what to do, and they'd have all the equipment. She found the number in the white pages on her phone and called them. A woman called Christine said they'd be out as soon as possible. Jasmine couldn't stay, but she said she would call them later to see how they went. The pelican would probably stay around the ramp while the fishing boats kept coming in, and there seemed to be quite a few today.

As soon as she arrived home she knew something was wrong. Her mum looked worried.

'Jaz. The police were here. They wanted to see you.'

'It's okay, Mum. Nothing serious.' She wasn't going to say anything to her mum about the packet yet, but now she had to.

'I found a small plastic bag of powder down by the boat ramp and I handed it in to the police just in case it was drugs.'

'God Jaz. You shouldn't have touched the stuff. They might think you're involved.' She handed the card to Jasmine. 'They want you to call.'

'I'll call straightway. It's nothing Mum. Don't freak.'

The police had tested the powder and it was cocaine. They wanted Jasmine to come to the station to give prints. She knew they'd be probing for more information. The police station was a new building, built alongside the court house on the outskirts of the town. Like most new government buildings it was all glass and aluminium on the outside but not as imposing inside. There was the usual bland reception area with halls and doorways leading to who knows where. She wondered about the poor souls interrogated behind those walls. She felt guilty just walking in the main door, so she could imagine how tough it must be for some people. The older policeman she'd seen the other day, Sergeant Gray, led her into a small room to the left of the front counter, sat her down and offered her coffee.

'Did you see anyone around that area, any cars, anyone acting suspiciously?' he asked looking over the top of his glasses.

'I already told you the place was deserted. No one bothers going there at night except for a few fishermen.'

'And you,' he said raising his bushy eyebrows. 'Tell me again why you were there.' He sat back in the chair and folded his arms.

'I go there for the quiet. A place to think. But I go there a lot on my days off. I take photos of the pelicans, so I can paint pictures of them later on.'

'A young woman like you shouldn't be hanging around there at night on your own.' He stood and adjusted his belt. 'We'll be stepping up patrols. We are aware of drug activity around there, and we really want to nail it. Let us know if you see or hear anything else. Come this way now and we'll do those prints.'

Susie was distracted all day Friday. She smiled and chatted with the old people, gave out medication, made beds, bathed patients and fed them, but this meeting with Doug was running through her mind. She'd had a few short relationships since she moved to the coast but she found she was too busy, too tired. She thought of Doug in the lonely times when the kids weren't there, when she'd reach out to the other side of the bed, dreaming he was still there, and she'd wrap her arms around herself sobbing through the emptiness. She remembered the good times they had as a family in Sydney. They'd met at a friend's party and she was instantly attracted to his confident manner, his quirky aloof attitude and the mystery of him. She loved his man smell, the strength and warmth of him. God how she missed that. They started out okay, but then his marketing company crashed and he was left with a bruised ego. Susie started work at St George's Hospital to help with the finances, but Doug started drinking more and more, and then came the late nights and weekends he was away. Susie was worried but he said everything was fine, that he was setting up work contracts. Then she saw him in the city with Cindy. She was devastated. Although her intuition told her something was not right, she just didn't want to believe it. Now she was seeing him again she wasn't sure what would pan out. He might have really changed for the worse, or as he said, he might be trying to put the past behind him, make amends.

That night Jasmine decided to drive to the park after helping Amanda choose her wedding bouquet at the florist's shop. The wedding was only a week away now so she'd offered to help where she could. Amanda was getting excited but also stressed. She'd been going to a Boot Camp so that she could lose some kilos before her big day, but this seemed to be really exhausting her. She really should have worked up to it, started months ago. But that wasn't Amanda's style.

Jasmine parked in a side street where she could get a good view of the boat ramp. There were no street lights here so her little bottle green Honda would not stand out. *What am I waiting for? This is crazy. I could be home watching tellie or chatting to friends.* She crouched down low and plugged her ear phones in. She didn't have to wait long. The same white rental car pulled up, followed by a noisy bomb car. It looked like the same two guys, but she was back further this time and couldn't be sure. They exchanged backpack-type bags and the bomb car rattled off. The man who looked like her dad threw his bag in the boot and reversed out of his parking spot. She started her engine and eased her little car into the main street following the rental car. She kept a safe distance, but she had to concentrate as she didn't want to lose him. He drove right into her street. *What? Why's he going here?* She slowed at the corner and watched him pull into her driveway. *God he's got a cheek. What will Mum say?* She decided to wait for a while. It would be a bit obvious if she followed him in.

She drove to the end of the street, pulled over and waited about ten minutes before going back to the house. They both turned to face her when she walked in. Her mum looked flushed, excited. Jasmine looked from one to the other.

'Jaz,' her mum said, 'Doug's come for a chat. We were just going out for some fish and chips. Do you want some?'

'No thanks. I ate something in town,' Jasmine said trying to avoid Doug's eyes.

'Hey Jaz, why did you want to contact me the other day?' Doug asked, as Susie went off to get her bag.

'What...what do you mean?'

'I had to book the car a few more days and the girl at the Rentals said you'd called. Couldn't contact me.'

'Oh. I'd lost your number and I thought I'd find out where you were staying. I wanted to see you before you left.'

'Susie has my number. Couldn't you have asked her?'

'I...' Jasmine turned as Susie came back and grabbed the keys. Doug gave her a strange look and followed Susie out.

Jasmine felt cemented to the spot. He made her feel so creepy. She didn't like the way he looked at her. She heard them drive off so now was her chance. He'd left his keys on the table. What a piece of luck. She dashed out, peered up the street and approached the rental car. She managed to push the button for the boot after a few attempts and then she stood frozen looking at the bag. *What am I doing? He could come back any minute.* She pulled the zip a fraction but it was stiff. She opened it a few centimetres but the light in the boot was too dim. She inched it further, further. Then she saw it was filled with bundles of cash. Lots of it. Drug money? Her heart nearly leapt out of her chest. *Shit.* She zipped the bag shut and slammed the boot lid. She checked the car was locked and raced inside, placing the keys exactly where he left them.

She went straight to her bedroom and closed the door. *What now? What the fuck am I going to do? Mum was looking cosy with him. I'll have to tell her. She can't be involved in this. I can't be involved in this.*

She plonked herself on the bed with her laptop. *Some online chatting will help me forget all this rubbish.*

She heard voices and someone went to the bathroom. There were more voices, then a car door thudded and a vehicle drove off. Her mum tapped on her bedroom door and asked if she could come in. She was beaming and holding out a thick envelope.

'Go on Jaz. It's for you from Doug. There's one for Stephen too.'

Jasmine wouldn't take it. 'What is it?'

'Go on,' Susie insisted coming closer to the bed. 'It's money...and lots of it.'

Jasmine felt her face drain. 'No way. I'm not touching it,' she said as she shuffled further up the bed. Susie sat down.

'I know how you must feel, but Doug wants to try again. He's changed. He wants to help you kids.' She sighed. 'And guess what? He's taking me on a date.'

'What? You're kidding right?' Jasmine put her hands over her face. 'No. No Mum. Don't go there. Please.' Jasmine was shaking her head and close to tears.

'Look, just think about it. That money would be a big help. It would help your car payments. You could buy new clothes, even jewellery.'

Jasmine jumped up, dumped the laptop and held her mouth. 'I have to go to the bathroom.' And she rushed down the hall.

I'll have to tell Mum now. Otherwise she'll get sucked in. I can't let that happen. The bastard. He's just trying to buy us back. But if I tell Mum, then what do we do? Tell the cops and then live in fear as informants? Not tell the cops and let him get away with it? And then there's the money. We are already incriminated. Shit. Shit. Shit.

Jasmine washed her face and confronted her mum. She told her about the meetings at the boat ramp, how she contacted the rental company, how she'd followed the car here. Her mum was visibly shocked but still in disbelief.

'That was a dangerous thing to do Jaz. But you don't really know if he's involved in anything shady.'

'But Mum. I haven't finished. I waited till you'd both gone for fish and chips and I opened the boot of his car. There was a bag, Mum. A bag full of cash.' Jasmine started chewing a nail.

'Shit,' Susie said. 'That changes everything. How could I be so naive? I can't believe it.' She paused. 'But maybe there's a legitimate explanation. We don't really know if it was drug money.'

'Get real. What else would it be? No one picks up that amount of cash at night, at a secret meeting. And there's the bag of cocaine. Isn't that enough evidence?'

Susie stood up. 'We will have to think long and hard about this. Don't make any rash decisions. Let's have a coffee...and we definitely won't mention this to Stephen.'

SEVEN

Brad stepped out of the lift into the stark hospital corridor and smelt the memory of childhood operations. He'd never forget the broken arm, and the tonsil operation when he was about six. They'd put him in a hospital gown and his mum said he was most embarrassed. 'I look like a girl,' he'd said to her. His mum always remembered those funny things.

Cheryl was approaching, her head down. She looked frailer than he'd ever seen her before. The faded blue dress she was wearing, hung loosely from her bony frame.

'Mum,' Brad said. Cheryl jumped.

'Thank God you're here. I'm just ducking out for a smoke.' She fidgeted with her hands.

'How is he?'

'Well he's on some drug that calms him down. But he's angry. Can't understand why he's in here.' She paused and chewed her lip. 'Do something for me Brad. Don't pay any attention to what he says. Let it go over your head.' Cheryl walked off and pressed the lift button. Brad moved off in the opposite direction headed to room number seven.

He stopped at the door. The bed looked lonely in the sparse room. He guessed there was no furniture for safety reasons. His father looked like he was sleeping, his head tilted sideways. His once solid frame seemed to sink into the bed and his grey hair stuck out at weird angles. His round face was flushed and blotchy. His hands flopped by his side. He turned as Brad approached and he blinked a few times, trying to focus.

'What do you want?'

'Dad. It's Brad. How are you going?'

'What do you think?' He propped himself higher. 'Don't know why they put me here. I can't even get out to do a piss.'

'They know what's best.'

'What would they know? What would you know? You weren't there.' He glared at Brad. Brad hoped his mother would return soon.

'You're useless too,' he rambled on. 'You have to be tough like I was. Go to Nam and fight.' Then he appeared to shake his head, close his eyes and whimper. 'But what was it for? No one gives a fuck.' He paused and spluttered. 'Where's your mother? She was getting the bloody nurse. I can't stand the noise in here.' He put his hands over his ears and screwed up his bulbous face. 'Stop it! Stop the bloody noise!'

He let his father rant and rave for a while. He walked to the window and stared out, clenching his hands behind his back. Soon Cheryl rushed in and grabbed John's hands. 'John, John. It's okay. The nurse will be here soon.'

Brad moved over and rubbed his mum's arm up and down. He saw the tears pooling in her eyelids.

'I've gotta go. See you later,' he said. He bent to kiss his dad but John started yelling again. Brad left the room, not knowing what to do.

What the hell am I supposed to do? I can't help him. He hasn't any time for me. I was never good enough. They're his demons. Trouble is, we're the ones trying to deal with it. Poor Mum. As far back as he could remember his father had always been a moody erratic man. How his mum put up with it, he'd never know. She was brought up a strict Catholic and she didn't believe in divorce. She was determined to stick by him no matter what. But how much could she stand? She'd taken up smoking and she was a shadow of her former self. If this was what going to war did, he didn't ever want any part in it. That's why he needed the escape the trawler and fishing gave him. Get away for a bit. It was all too much sometimes.

He drove home with a heavy head and a feeling of anger. Why did his father treat him this way? He acted like a real arsehole sometimes and part of him wished he'd just leave. Get out of their lives.

When he got home his mind was in turmoil. He needed a stiff drink but he filled a glass with water first. There was a soft tap at the door.

'Well, it's the Pelican Girl,' Brad said as he smiled and leant on the door frame.

'Is Andy home?'

'Not yet. But you can come in. He shouldn't be too long. He said his chick would be picking him up. But I didn't realise it would be you.'

Jasmine was surprised to see Brad so clean, so well-dressed. She wondered why. Must've been out somewhere.

'Can I get you a drink?'

Jasmine shook her head. Now that he had short sleeves, she could see a tattoo on his upper arm, a wrap-around wave design. He really was yummy looking but she still felt uneasy. He sat across from her on a single lounge chair drinking a glass of water.

'How long have you known Andy?' he asked. She looked pretty sexy with her hair down, strands swirling around her porcelain face, and the fitted top accentuating her cute breasts. His eyes went down to her feet, clad only in thongs. He could get down right now and kiss that pelican tattoo on her delicate ankle.

'Just since he started at the zoo.'

Brad nodded. 'That's right. Brad said you work there in the photo place.'

'Yes,' Jasmine said scanning the room, feeling self conscious with Brad looking at her so intensely.

'Jasmine... It is Jasmine right?' he said. Jasmine nodded. 'Can I give you a bit of advice? Just be careful with Andy okay.'

'What do you mean?' Jasmine faced him and frowned.

'Well. Andy's...he's a pot head. And lately he's been hanging out with drug losers. I think you should be careful.'

Jasmine was flabbergasted. 'I think I'm old enough to judge for myself. It's none of your business.'

'Fine,' he said shrugging his shoulders.

Jasmine stood up. She felt sick, light-headed. 'Can I use your bathroom?'

'Sure. Down the hall on the left.' Brad rinsed his glass and pulled a beer from the fridge. He started scratching around in the pantry for some biscuits or chips.

Jasmine was fuming. *Could you believe it? Giving me a lecture. What a nerve. Plenty of people smoke pot.*

After she washed her hands Jasmine stopped at the open door of one of the bedrooms and peered in. She could hear Brad banging dishes around in the kitchen. She saw Andy's zoo uniform draped over the end of the messy double bed. She took a few steps in. The room smelt of pot and sleep. A guitar and surf board leant in a corner and there was a backpack and baseball cap tossed near the door. There was an upturned crate used as a bedside table, and on top was a watch, a pile of coins, an ipod and loose papers. A laptop was on top of an old chest of drawers which was losing paint and missing several knobs. There were a couple of posters stuck to the wall. One from a bike magazine, showed a big breasted girl wearing very little clothing, sitting astride a new KTM and pouting at the camera. Jasmine knew a bit about bikes because her last boyfriend Scott was into them big time. *Bloody Scott. Why does his image keep taunting me.* The other one was of a heavy metal band from a music magazine. She wasn't sure who they were. She wasn't into that sort of music.

She walked up the hall and grabbed her bag. Brad was texting on his mobile.

'Tell Andy I'll meet him at the pub.'

'Okay,' Brad said walking over to the door. *God he was cute. And those eyes. What was he wearing? The smell was delicious.*

'Jasmine. Look after yourself, okay?'

She smiled, glanced back and nearly tripped on the top step.

Then he said, 'Are you eating properly? You don't want to spoil that model figure by getting too bony.' He had a sparkle in his eye but Jasmine's face fell. She stormed off. *Too bony. What a moron.*

Jasmine waited for over an hour at the pub. It was the usual Saturday night, busy and noisy. Her friends Sara and Zoe spotted her and came over for a chat.

'Can you play Goal Defence this week?' Sara said. 'Nat's sick. She's not going to make it.'

'Sure,' Jasmine said. She played netball with her friends from school in the hall at the Sports Club. She enjoyed the exercise and the company. They chatted for a while and then Sara and Zoe went off to meet their boyfriends at the bar.

There was still no sign of Andy. She was about to order a salad when he arrived flushed in the face and apologising profusely. He was distracted, jumpy. Then his phone went off. He apologised again and walked over to the exit door. *God he's one busy boy. Always in demand.* Maybe Brad was right after all. Andy had probably been on the weed. He was certainly more animated than usual, and his eyes were wide and staring. Jasmine sipped her drink and gazed towards the ocean.

They ate their meals in silence. She picked at her salad but Andy was wolfing his food down.

'You're quiet tonight,' he said wiping his mouth with the serviette.

'What?' Jasmine turned to face him. 'I'm sorry. I've had a crazy week.'

'Well taking koala photos can't be all that stressful.'

'It's not work.' She paused. 'It's my dad. He turned up...from Sydney. We hadn't seen him for over eleven years and I guess it just stirred up emotions I'd put away.'

'Yeah. Well that sounds tough.'

'And there's all the wedding stuff. I've been helping Amanda because she's started to stress about it all.'

'Is she having a hen's night?'

'Yes. The bridesmaids usually organise it, but she's not having bridesmaids, so Megan and I are doing it.'

'That'd be fun. What have you got planned?'

'We're meeting at her place first for pre-dinner drinks and games, then we'll be going to Gino's Theatre Restaurant.'

'Cool. They get everyone involved in the music and dancing. Hey what are the games you chicks play at the hen's?' Andy asked, a sparkle in his eye.

'Ah. That's private stuff,' Jasmine said smiling.

'Come on.'

'Well, one game is like Pin the Tail on the Donkey,' Jasmine said a smirk on her face. 'Except it's Pin the Penis on the Guy.'

'Ouch,' Andy laughed as he squeezed his legs together.

When they'd finished their meals and drinks Andy suggested a walk on the beach.

'Why don't we drive around to the point and walk up the beach from the car park? It's much more private...and romantic,' he said kissing her neck and snuggling up.

The walking track along the canal was deserted at this time of night. The cyclonic weather had abated and the coast was now experiencing the calm and clear skies that it was famous for. Jasmine looked up at the white lighthouse on the point, its lifesaving beam turning rhythmically and flashing out to sea. She often thought of it as a symbol of hope and stability in the turmoil and rush of the ocean. The waves smashed onto the distant rocks but the shallow water of the little cove whispered in and out, as gentle and soothing as a lover.

'Isn't it peaceful?'Jasmine said. 'I just love the beach...and the birds.'

'Hey. What happened with that pelican you were telling me about? The one with the hook in its neck?' Andy asked.

'He's going to be okay. I rang the Rescue Service. They managed to remove the hook and line. But his leg was lacerated so they've got him on antibiotics. I'm going to see George tomorrow. That's what they called him...George. Do you want to come?'

'I'll give it a miss I think. You can deal with George.'

'How's Bertha going?'

'Fine. She's very easy to deal with. Not like most females I know,' Andy scoffed.

Jasmine pushed him hard and he stumbled, nearly falling in the water. She ran off, flicking the sand up and glancing back. Andy steadied himself and joined in the race. He grabbed her, tackled her and they fell together in a laughing heap. They rolled around on the sand in their urgent embrace, kissing passionately. They were entwined as one, each not daring to relax in case the spell was broken. They explored each other's bodies enjoying the warmth, the sensations, the sensuality. Slowly they discarded pieces of clothing. Jasmine had never felt such tingling, such overwhelming pleasure. She felt as if she was in another place, another time, nothing else mattered. The breakers roared and crashed while they rode together on an ocean of ecstasy, pulling at each other's hair and skin, moaning and calling out with no boundaries, no inhibitions.

They walked back to the car in a state of contentment. Jasmine had not felt this intimacy for a long time and she sighed as she leant on him and breathed him in.

She really liked Andy. He was fun to be with, but Brad's warning remained stuck in her head and she was constantly on the lookout for any indication of drug-affected behaviour or involvement with the drug world. It was the constant phone calls and texts that irked her. He always seemed secretive about it, moving away from her when he was deep in conversation. But that was nothing really. Why worry?

'Would you like to come to Amanda's wedding with me? she asked.

'When is it?'

'Saturday. The ceremony's here at the park overlooking the sea. Then they're having a reception at the Yacht Club.'

'Cool. That'd cost a bit at that place.'

'It's her in-laws. They wanted it. They're into sailing. They own a huge yacht...among other things.'

'Lucky girl,' Andy said.

'Yeah. But money often means power. And Amanda doesn't like to be controlled. She's an independent spirit.'

EIGHT

It was some foreign film with sub-titles, the usual poor Saturday night viewing choices. Susie was staring at the TV screen, her eyes blurred, her mind numb. *How could something like this happen? It can't be Doug. It's some other guy. They're lying. He was just here. This can't be happening. He was taking me on a date. Now that's gone forever.* She thought back to Sydney, the trips to Watson's Bay, walking in the Blue Mountains, camping in the National Park. The kids were happy. *It's not bloody fair.* She heard the dull thud as a car door closed and she wiped her face and straightened her back.

'Mum. Why are you still up?' Jasmine said. Then she saw Susie's streaked face and swollen eyes. She sat down beside her. 'God Mum what's wrong? What is it?' she said wrapping her arm around her mother's shoulders.

Susie sobbed into Jasmine's shoulder. 'It's your dad. Doug. They think it's him ...they found him murdered.'

'God no. Where? When?'

'Someone found him in his hotel room this morning.' She kept shaking her head. 'It can't be him Jaz, it just can't.'

'Oh no, Mum,' Jasmine said quietly. Suddenly she felt sick. 'How did you find out?'

'The police called earlier. They'd contacted Doug's parents in Newcastle and they told the police down there about you kids...and me.' Susie added another scrunched up tissue to the growing pile on the coffee table. They sat in silence for a while trying to come to terms with it all.

'Does Stephen know?'

'Yes. I told him. He didn't say anything. He feels bitter about how we were just left. He's in his room. He was on the computer for a while but I think he's gone to sleep now.' Then Susie turned to face Jasmine. 'The police want us to come to the station in the morning to give statements.'

'What for? It's nothing to do with us. How can they think we had anything to do with it?'

Susie took a deep breath. 'They want to track his movements and talk to all the people he came in contact with.'

Jasmine chewed at her fingernail. 'Do you think we'll need to tell them about the drugs, the money?'

Susie nodded. 'If we don't we could get into deep trouble. They'd probably find out sooner or later.'

'Shit. The bloody idiot. Why did we have to get dragged into this? And we've got some of his filthy money.'

'He was trying to change. It's not fair. It's just not fair.'

'How about I make us both a hot chocolate. Maybe that'll help us sleep.'

Susie doubted if that would work but she just nodded and sighed.

Jasmine sat on the hard wooden seat in the police station's reception area, staring ahead and wondering how her mother was going in the interview. This room was cold and sterile and it smelt like an old library. She looked around at the faded posters on the wall, the dark wood panelling, the old light fittings, the scuffed floor. This station was in an old building, not revamped and modern like the Caloundra one. The phone rang and a young female constable answered it and spoke softly. An old lady shuffled in. 'Hello Dear,' she said to the girl at the counter who'd just finished her call. 'Can you help me? My little dog's gone missing. He's my best friend. He's all I've got since Herb died.' Jasmine looked down at the pile of magazines but they were outdated, and she couldn't read right now anyhow. People came and went, and the phone kept ringing, but she took little notice. The old lady was still going on about the dog. She was gazing at the scuffed vinyl floor and barely noticed when someone sat beside her.

'Hello Miss Pelican.'

She snapped out of her dreamy state and focussed on the man beside her. Brad.

'God. You gave me a fright,' she said.

'Well I don't look that bad do I?' He smirked. She noticed bruising and a cut above one eye.

'What happened to you?' she asked.

'I had a fight with a door.' He paused and watched her puzzled look. 'No. Some druggo decked me last night outside the tavern.'

'Are you okay? Is that why you're here?'

'Yeah I'm okay. But the coppers wanted me to make a statement. They want to nail the guy. He's done this before.'

' The rotten bugger. But you probably provoked it.'

'Look at me,' Brad said. 'Do I look like I would start a fight?' He gave her that witty look of his.

'You'd be Mr Nice Guy right?'

'And why are you here might I ask? I can't imagine you in trouble with the law.'

Jasmine wrapped her arms around herself and lowered her head. She was barely audible. 'My father just died. He was murdered.'

'I wish someone murdered my father,' Brad looked away and mumbled.

'What?' Jasmine said. Then she continued. 'He wasn't really my father...I mean we hardly saw him. He deserted us.'

'How do they know it was him?'

'They told us...it's my dad.'

'Did he live around here?'

'No. Sydney. But he was up here on business, or so he said.'

'Did you see him while he was here?'

'Yeah. But it was awkward.'

A young female constable came out of the hallway and called Jasmine's name. Brad got up to go. She'd felt his closeness, his breath, but at the same time he irritated her.

'Can you not tell Andy yet?'

'That's your business,' he said with a shrug and he walked off.

'Jasmine. Can you come on through please?' Jasmine followed the woman down a hall. A couple of men walked past with briefcases and folders in their hands, deep in conversation. The woman led her to a small room at the end of the corridor, a cool breeze creeping towards them. Even with the chill in the air she felt clammy and she wiped her hands on the side of her jeans. She was scared. What if she said the wrong thing? What had her mother told them?

There were two detectives in dark suits in the room. It was a bit daunting, just a table and chairs and the video camera mounted above it. A plain white clock on the wall frowned down on her. Her mouth felt dry and she kept fidgeting with her hands. They introduced themselves and asked her if she'd like a drink. They went through the formalities, full name, age, address, occupation. She felt as if the room had a thousand eyes that were all boring holes into her.

'What relation was Douglas Bennett to you?' the younger man asked. She noticed he had a coffee stain on his white shirt. He was clean shaven and his hair was cut short, very short. It was so short in fact that you couldn't tell its true colour. His eyes seemed to look right through her. The older man was taking notes.

'He was my father,' Jasmine said.

'Can you speak a little louder please? Now we believe that you lived apart from your father. He lived in Sydney is that right?'

'Yes.'

'He made this trip to the Sunshine Coast to see you and your brother. Is that correct?'

'Yes sort of. He told me he was coming on business and we arranged a meeting.'

'Did he visit often?'

'No. This was the first time since the divorce, since I was about ten.'

'When was the last time you saw him?'

'When he came to see Mum. That was on Friday night.'

'Can you tell me what time that was?'

'It was around dinner time. He and Mum went off to get fish and chips.'

'And by dinner time you mean what? Six? Seven?'

'It would have been around seven o'clock.'

'When did he leave your house?'

'When he and Mum came back from having their meal. That would have been close to eight.'

'How would you describe your relationship with your father?'

'I hardly knew him. He left when I was ten.'

'And did you see him at all during that time? Were there any phone calls? Cards ? Letters?'

Jasmine shook her head. 'No.' She was starting to feel faint. She brushed her damp hair off her face. She wished they'd hurry up.

'That must have upset you. A father who's deserted you?'

'At first it did, but later we moved up here and we got on with our lives. What else could we do?'

He sat back in his chair and loosened his tie.

'Jasmine we've spoken to your mother and we believe you have information that may help us in our investigations.'

Jasmine looked from one detective to the other. 'Could I have a glass of water please?'

She proceeded to tell them all about the meetings she'd seen, the plastic bag, the descriptions of the men and their cars, the money in the boot and the money Doug had offered them. The questioning went on for over an hour and Jasmine was relieved to get out in the fresh air.

Bloody hell. All those questions. It's as if we have some part in this. We're the ones who are made to feel guilty. I wish I'd never seen Doug or his dirty money. God I hope that's the end to it.

She texted Andy and said she was coming over. 'I need 2 c u ,' she typed.

She pulled up at the flat and had to park in the street because a gleaming red Commodore sedan took pride of place beside Brad's black ute. *Wow. I wonder where the old bomb is ? Andy said he'd be home. Must be visitors.*

Andy appeared in the doorway a cigarette in his mouth.

'Hey Princess. What do you think?' He leapt down the steps, stubbing his cigarette on the railing. He grabbed her and swung her around. 'Come for a spin my sweet.' He opened the passenger door.

'What? Is this yours?' she asked. He gave her a gentle push and she fell into the comfort of the plush seats. Jasmine gasped.

'Andy. Wow. This is gorgeous.'

'Yep. I'm coming up in the world.' He started the engine. 'Where to, Princess Jasmine?'

'Andy how could you afford this ?'

'I've got a job now remember. And I was lucky. My oldies helped me out.'

'Great. It's really cool.'

They drove to the Point Cartwright, Andy pointing out the many electronic buttons and up-to-date functions of the new car. They pulled up at the park and Andy leant over and kissed her. She pulled back.

'Andy. I've got something to tell you.'

'This sounds serious,' he said with a quirky look on his face.

'You remember I told you about my dad. How he came up from Sydney and I met up with him.'

'Yeah,' Andy said.

'Well. He's been found dead...murdered.'

'What? You're kidding.' Andy looked intensely at Jasmine then stared ahead. 'Where was this?'

'He was stabbed in his hotel room.' Jasmine stared out across the canal. Squealing children ran around the playground, and she watched as a couple of fishing boats motored past.

Andy had his hand on his forehead. 'Oh God. That's not your father? The murder I read about in the paper this morning?' He lit a cigarette and took a deep breath. 'Far out.'

After a while Jasmine said, 'And I've been at the police station. They asked hundreds of questions.'

'Why? What would you know? How could you help?'

'They wanted to know his last movements, who he saw, our relationship, that sort of thing.'

He reached over and cuddled her. 'You poor thing. That must have been terrible. What can we do to take your mind off it?'

'I want to see George,' Jasmine said. 'Let's go to the Rescue Centre.'

The Rescue Centre was situated about 15 kilometres from Caloundra. It was tucked away in a quiet rural area where there were only a few scattered houses. They travelled through thick forest and towering eucalypts and followed a dirt track to the main building which was set back from the main road and surrounded by a tall timber fence. They entered through the main gate and followed a path which bordered a large lake. Several pelicans were snoozing or grooming themselves around its edges. A couple slipped into the water and started swimming towards them.

'Sorry guys. We don't have any fish,' Jasmine said. She turned to Andy. 'It's strange seeing them here in the bush. I'm used to seeing them by the beach.'

They met Christine, the manager, and she told them that the pelicans on the lake were there to stay. She said they had problems which made it impossible for them to be released. Some of them couldn't fly.

'It must cost a lot. All that fish you have to get for them,' Jasmine said.

'It sure does,' Christine replied. 'We rely totally on donations. We show groups of people through and they give money, or sometimes we give talks out in the community and we raise money that way. It's important to educate people about protecting our precious wildlife.'

Andy was reading a poster on the wall. It was a chart with pictures of all the species of seabird found on the Sunshine Coast. There were other pictures too, and pelican photos.

'So where's George?' Jasmine said.

'He's in the Observation Area. Come and see.'

George was strutting around in a large cage and he waddled up to the wire when he saw that he had visitors.

'Hi Georgie. How are you hey?' Jasmine said bending down to his level. She noticed the dressing in his leg. 'So he had a sore leg too?'

'Yes. The fishing line had cut through to the bone. It would have been very painful. Every time he moved, it sliced in deeper.'

'He was lucky you found him Jaz,' Andy said.

'When will you release him?' Jasmine asked.

'Soon. He's doing really well, so probably this week sometime.'

'Do you think I could come? Could I see you release him?'

'Sure, I'll give you a call.'

They gave Christine a small donation and headed back to Caloundra.

'They do a great job there. Not many people realise what hard work it is, and the cost involved,' Jasmine said.

'Maybe they should advertise more,' Andy said.

'Yeah but that costs money too.'

They rode in silence for a while.

'So did that take your mind off things?' Andy asked.

'Um-m. It was good to get away. But I have to go home now and see how Mum and Stephen are.'

'Did the police say what might have happened?'

'No. They don't tell us anything.'

NINE

Susie was hanging out a load of washing when Jasmine returned home. She helped peg out the last of the items.

'So how was your interview Mum? Did they really grill you too?'

'Yes. It was pretty full-on. They know it all now, so hopefully they'll leave us alone.'

'Do they think they know who might be responsible? Did they say anything more about the drug thing?' Jasmine asked as they walked inside.

'All they said was that they'd been doing surveillance for drug activity in this area. They have several persons of interest, but they need more evidence.' She paused. 'Bloody Doug. Why the hell did he get involved in drugs? Now look where it puts us. I have nothing to look forward to.'

'You have us,' Jasmine said. 'We would be more reliable than he could ever have been. Be realistic Mum.'

She continued, 'What about the cash? Was it still in the car?'

'They said not. But they think whoever murdered Doug was after that money. They've fingerprinted the car, and the hotel has cameras everywhere, so they are confident they'll get someone soon.' Susie went to the fridge. 'I'm exhausted. Let's have a wine.'

'Did they question Stephen too?'

'Yes. But I can't get anything out of him. He took off surfing with Mark.' They both sat back in the lounge sipping their wine and nibbling on savoury biscuits and cheese. Jasmine put her feet up and curled them under her.

'Mum do you think we're in danger? Will these drug guys come after us?'

Susie sat up straight. 'Shit. I never thought of that really.' She slipped back down again. 'I can't see why that would happen. We were not involved. Doug was only with us briefly.'

'But they might think we were involved. They might think we know something.'

That night they made sure all the windows and doors were well secured. Jasmine tossed and turned in her bed, and when she finally dozed off it was a disturbed sleep. A dog's bark pierced the night air and Jasmine woke with a start, her eyes springing open like a Holland blind. There was scratching at her window. She froze. Luckily the blind was pulled right down so whoever or whatever was out there could not see in. *It's just a dream. It's okay. It's nothing.* She rolled over. There it was again. Someone was trying to prise open her window. She was out of there like a gun bullet, straight to her mother's room.

'Mum, Mum,' she whispered urgently. She shook the sleeping mound. 'I think there's someone out there. Outside my room.'

Susie sat up, groaned and rubbed her eyes. 'What? Where?' Susie said.

They both tiptoed into Jasmine's bedroom, clinging to each other.

'I can't hear anything,' Susie whispered. They edged over to the blind and peeked out of the crack at the side. The street on this side of the house was fairly light because of a street lamp nearby. There was only one camellia bush close to the window, the rest of the yard was just lawn. There was no one to be seen.

'It was probably the wind in that bush,' Susie said. But Jasmine was not convinced. She'd never heard that scraping before.

'I'm coming into your room.'

'I don't think I'd be much protection,' Susie said and they both giggled.

Jasmine was thankful it was her day off because she felt terrible. She had dark rings under her eyes and her cheeks looked hollow. Amanda needed help with the little gifts she was putting on each wedding table, so Jasmine went to her house for the morning. Afterwards she walked down by the Passage and took more photos of the boats and the birds. She got a good shot of three pelicans sitting on one of the blue rowboats that were moored near the jetty. She texted Andy. 'c u 2 nite. xx u.' He said he'd come around after dinner.

She turned the corner into her street and her mouth fell open. *What? What now?*

The police were at her house. Two men in suits were at the front door and they came down the stairs as she drove in.

'Jasmine,' the older man said. 'You remember us. Detective Baker and Detective Rowe.' They were the same detectives who interviewed her at the station. The older, stocky one was Baker and the younger one with the very short hair was Detective Rowe. He held out a sheet of paper. 'We have a search warrant for this place. Is anyone else home?'

'I...No Mum's at work but she'll be home soon.'

'That's fine. We can start without her. James could you ring her?' He opened up his notebook and gave the other detective the number. 'Tell her what's happening. She should be here.'

Jasmine was speechless. She stood with her mouth open.

'Um. Detective,' she finally said. 'What...what's this all about?'

'We are searching the premises. It may help in our investigation.'

'How? What are you looking for?'Jasmine said, following the men up the stairs.

'We can't say. But we have to follow a lead.'

Jasmine opened the door and the police filed in, the two men in suits and two other officers. She noticed they were wearing gloves. *Hurry up Mum. I can't do this on my own. It freaks me out. What the hell are they looking for?*

Susie turned up ten minutes later. She rushed into the house. 'What's going on?' she demanded of Detective Baker, the older man standing in the kitchen.

'A search ma'am. We're looking for more evidence.'

'Evidence? Evidence of what?'

'We will tell you when we find it,' he said smugly. Susie stormed down the hall. Jasmine hadn't seen her mum this mad before. The police were in the bedrooms now, going through drawers, lifting up mattresses.

'You won't find anything,' she growled. 'We had nothing to do with any of this. Why can't you just fuck off and leave us alone.' After a while, the men gathered in the kitchen and the ones who'd done the search shook their heads.

'We need your car keys,' Rowe said. 'Both of you.'

'God I can't believe this. I can't fuckin' believe this,' Susie said flopping on the lounge. The house held its breath for several minutes as the police did their search. Then she heard their footsteps, and as she glanced at the door her face went white. Detective Rowe was holding up a backpack in his gloved hand.

'We found it in your boot Jasmine. Is it yours?'

'No'. Jasmine shook her head and swallowed. Her blood went cold. It was the bag. The money bag she'd seen in her Dad's car.

'Is this the bag you saw in your father's car last Friday night?'

'Yes. I think. It looks similar,' Jasmine said. The detective walked over to Jasmine with an arrogant look on his face. He opened the zip right in front of her and held the bag open.

'Does this look familiar?' he asked. 'All this cash?'

Jasmine nearly fainted. She grabbed a chair and slid into it.

'I didn't put it there. I never touched it.'

'If it wasn't you, then who do you think put it there?' Rowe asked.

'I don't know. How would I know?'

Susie stood up and butted in. 'Someone's put it there Detective, but it wasn't my daughter. Jasmine would never be involved in anything like that.'

Rowe turned to her. 'Then Ms Bennett, how do you think it got there?' He raised his eyebrows.

'I don't fuckin' know. Who bloody knows?' Susie said throwing her arms up in exasperation.

'Did either of you see Doug Bennett go near Jasmine's car on that night?' he asked. They both shook their heads.

'Do you lock your car Jasmine?'

'Yes. I usually do.'

'Would he have been able to access the keys?'

'I guess. I leave them right there on the kitchen bench. But Mum was with him all the time. She would have seen him getting the keys.'

Susie frowned. 'That's right,' she said. 'We came back here after eating fish and chips. He came in briefly while I went to the toilet. That's all.' She spoke so quietly the detective could barely hear her.

'But you didn't see him with the keys, or going to the car, or maybe acting suspiciously?' Detective Baker said.

'Nup,' Susie said.

'Well the boot catch wasn't tampered with, so someone must have got the keys, or broken in through the car door. You have to think about who had access to those keys,' Baker said.

The detectives walked to the door to join their colleagues. 'Well thanks for your cooperation. We'll be in touch. And remember to call if you think of anything else,' Rowe said.

Susie rushed to her room and slammed the door. Jasmine curled up in the silent lounge.

Andy called around at about eight o'clock and Jasmine introduced him to Susie who had calmed down a little.

'I'm sorry about your loss. That must have been awful,' Andy said.

'Thanks,' Susie replied blankly. 'We're all a bit stressed at the moment.' She sighed. 'It's not the most welcoming and cheerful house. Sorry.'

'Mum. Andy and I are going out for a while,' Jasmine said.

They drove away from the house, both in quiet, subdued moods.

'Do you get down this way much?'Jasmine asked.

'No. But I probably will now,' Andy grinned.

Jasmine told him about her favourite spot. 'I want to take you there and you'll see how peaceful it is. I need a break from all the shit that's been happening.'

Andy followed Jasmine's directions. 'Is this it?'Andy asked as they drove past the park, only a few minutes from Jasmine's place.

'Yes,' she said. 'But drive up further to the boat ramp, then you don't have too far to walk to the water.' But Andy stopped the car.

'This'll do,' he snapped. Jasmine looked over. He was gripping the wheel and staring straight ahead.

'Are you okay?' she said moving closer to him.

'Sure, sure,' he said holding his stomach. 'I just had a stomach cramp. Must've been something I ate.'

'Well maybe you'd better go straight home.'

'No. No. It'll pass. Come on.' They walked down by the water and Andy lit a cigarette. He seemed preoccupied. He wasn't his usual jovial self.

'How was work today?' she asked.

'Yeah. It was fine,' he said staring out over the water. It was quiet except for the small waves lapping on the nearby pylons and the distant screeches of the terns on the sandbanks.

'Ask me about my day,' Jasmine said. He turned to face her.

'Okay.'

'Well it started out fine. I helped Amanda with the wedding gifts, I took some pelican photos, and then...'

'Then?'

'The police were at our house. They had a search warrant.'

'What? What were they after?'

'They didn't say but the horrible part is they did find something.' She paused. They both tensed.

'What?'

'A bag of cash. In the boot of my car. Can you believe it? I could be a wealthy woman. NOT.'

'How did that get there?'

'We don't know. But we have our suspicions. We think it was my father...Doug. We believe he was involved in some drug ring. He came around the other night and we think he might have planted it there.'

'Shit. That puts you in an awkward position.'

'I know and I'm scared. That bastard came up here, interfered in our lives, and now look what's happened.'

'Do they have any idea who killed him?'

'Not that I know of. But I'll bet they point the finger at us. You know...the money, the motive. We all hated him, except maybe Mum.'

'God that's creepy. Let's get out of here.' Andy stubbed his smoke and put the butt in a nearby bin as they turned back to the car. 'Why don't you come back to my place? It'll take your mind off things,' Andy said wrapping his arm around her. Jasmine said she would but she'd drive her car.

'I'll need to go home first and get some work clothes. I'll leave from your place in the morning.'

They went back to Andy's flat, and when she arrived, Andy loped down the stairs and grabbed her bag. He picked her up and carried her through to the bedroom.

'Andy,' she screeched and giggled, 'what are you doing?'

'Brad's out, so we have the place to ourselves,' he said smothering her with kisses and yanking at her clothes while he ripped his gear off. He threw her on the bed and straddled her, breathing heavily and exploring her with his mouth.

'God Andy you ...slow down,' she gasped. And then he drove into her with all his passion and pent-up emotions. Jasmine tried to move with him and clung to his strong back, but the tears came to her eyes, she sobbed and cried out. She stared at the ceiling as he pounded her She squeezed her eyes tight as he bit her neck and gripped her shoulders like a vice. What was wrong with him? It was if he was some wild, possessed animal. When he was done he groaned, rolled over and reached for his cigarettes. Jasmine faced the wall and cried silent tears.

TEN

At the zoo photo centre the next day Jasmine went about her work like a robot. The events of the past days had taken their toll and she was feeling terrible. She buttoned her shirt right up so the collar would hide the bruise on her neck. Andy had been his usual cheerful self this morning, but Jasmine felt a little jaded, used.

'Are you alright?'Megan asked. 'You don't look so good.'

'I'm fine,' Jasmine said half-smiling. 'A lot's happened lately. I'm a bit stressed that's all.'

She was packing up after the last snake photo session, when she felt as if everything was spinning around. She dropped to the floor. She could hear Megan's urgent voice, 'Jaz. Jaz. What's wrong? Wake up.'

She did wake up...in a doctor's surgery. A young, dark-haired female doctor was bending over her. 'Hello, Jasmine. I'm Doctor Archer. How are you feeling now? Let's try and sit you up a bit better.' The doctor and a nurse propped her up on the surgery bed and gave her a glass of water.

Just then Susie rushed in. 'Jasmine. God. What happened?'

'I'm fine Mum. Don't worry.' The doctor sat Susie down.

'Jasmine fainted at work. We're doing a few blood tests but we won't get the results till tomorrow. There are a few factors which could cause fainting.' She turned to Jasmine. 'Have you been under stress lately?'

'You could say that,' Susie replied.

'I'm concerned about your weight Jasmine,' Doctor Archer said. 'Have you been eating properly?' Jasmine nodded.

'No,' Susie said, 'she barely eats at all.'

Jasmine scowled at her mother. 'You wouldn't know Mum,' she said.

'I've got a fair idea and I think something has to be done before you fade away to nothing.'

Jasmine slipped off the bed. 'I'm fine really,' she said as they all moved to the door.

'I'll call with those results tomorrow,' the doctor said.

Jasmine noticed there were two missed calls on her phone. She rang the first one, Christine from the Bird Rescue Service. She said they'd be releasing George tomorrow afternoon at Military Jetty where all his mates hang out. Jasmine said she'd meet her there at 3.30pm.

The other call was from Detective Baker. He wanted her to come in as soon as possible that afternoon for further questioning.

'Not this afternoon, Jaz,' Susie said. 'You need to rest. Ring back and tell him another time.'

'No Mum, I'll go now. Get it over with.'

'Are you sure you're right to drive?' Susie said.

Jasmine rolled her eyes. 'M-u-m,' she said.

She arrived at the police station and braced herself. It was always unnerving coming here.

'Thanks for coming,' Detective Baker said. 'We just need some more information on the meetings you saw.' Jasmine nodded.

'We know about your father, but can you describe the other man?'

'Well he was tall, slim build and wearing a baseball cap.'

'When you say tall, how tall?' He stood up. 'As tall as me?'

'Yes sort of. Well he was taller than my dad and my dad is average height.'

'Can you describe his clothes?'

'Not really. The hat was a light colour but I couldn't see much. They were quite a distance away.'

'Any other features...moustache, beard, long hair, tattoos?'

'I'm pretty sure he was clean shaven, shortish hair.'

'What about the car? You said it was an old bomb.'

'Yes. It had a very noisy motor.'

'What colour, make, sedan, four wheel drive ?'

'It was a darkish colour, a sedan, don't know what make.'

'Anything else? Roof rack, stripes, mag wheels?' Baker looked up from his note book and chewed the end of his pen.

'There was a roof rack, I remember that.'

'Anything else?' Baker asked. Jasmine shook her head. Baker started to get up.

'Wait. I remember now. It had a lighter coloured boot, as if it was a replacement from the wreckers,' Jasmine said.

'Thanks Jasmine. You've been a good help. Just call if you remember anything else.'

They both pushed their chairs in and walked to the door.

'One last thing Jasmine. Your car. Who was in your house that night when the money was left in the boot? Who else might have had access to your keys?

' No one. Mum mentioned Dad but there was no one else.'

'No visitors? Boyfriend perhaps?'

'No.'

'And you didn't hear any tampering with your car or notice any forced entry?'

'None at all.'

As Jasmine drove home she had a weird feeling. *God I hope I'm not going to faint again.* She kept thinking about that meeting she saw, the first one when she found the packet. That car did have a distinctive boot. And then it became clear. She pulled up at the kerb. *Shit. That's where I've seen it before. At Andy's. It's Andy's bloody bomb car. What the hell am I going to do now? Bloody hell. That's all I need. Hang on... There's probably a logical explanation.* She took a deep breath and continued home. *Best to put it right at the back of my head.* She decided she would meet Andy for dinner. Maybe she could be subtle and find out more about the bomb car.

The next day the doctor called about the tests and told her she was slightly anaemic, and that she could get iron tablets or make sure she ate iron-rich foods. She said they were foods like red meats, salad greens, seafood and nuts, and that she could find the list on the internet.

'I also suggest you see a psychotherapist to help you deal with--- '

'I'm not going to some shrink,' Jasmine said through gritted teeth. 'I'm fine. I can deal with this myself.'

'Alright but I'd like to see you again soon to see how you're going.'

'Sure. Bye,' Jasmine said. *Bloody hell. As if I don't have enough going on. A shrink! I don't know why the weight is such an issue. If I get fat they'll worry about that too. Ya can't win.*

Jasmine arrived at Andy's place on Wednesday night but his car wasn't there. Brad was in the kitchen in his flannel shirt, dirty shorts and thongs.

'How are all the pelicans today?' he quipped.

'Catch any fish?' Jasmine asked. She was starting to get used to his silly remarks.

'Not many today. I went up the Maroochy River.' He wiped his hands on a towel and walked over.

'My grandfather liked to go there. We sometimes went to Chambers Island. It was great.'

'You'll have to come with me sometime. Fishing that is,' Brad said.

'Yeah right.' She started fidgeting and looking around. 'Where the hell is Andy?'

'He said he wouldn't be long. Sit down.'

'He's a busy boy. Lots of calls and meeting people,' Jasmine said.

'Yeah well I told you about some of his so called friends. And you have to wonder about that car.'

'What do you mean?' Jasmine said defensively.

'Well he normally wouldn't have that sort of money.'

'He said his parents helped him.'

'Yeah right. His mum died ages ago and the old boy is on an invalid pension. Lives down at the van park,' Brad said.

'Well he probably got a loan.'

'I doubt it,' Brad shrugged. He paused. 'Hey how did you get on at the cop shop the other day?'

'Okay. But a lot's happened since then. You wouldn't want to know.'

'Try me,' Brad said sitting opposite her. He looked at her with those deep eyes of his. She noticed the wound above his eye had almost healed. She wondered if she could trust him. He said strange things about Andy. Maybe he was jealous or something. Jasmine jumped up as she heard the Commodore drive in. 'Bye,' she said as she rushed out.

'I meant what I said about the fishing,' Brad called after her.

Jasmine jumped in beside Andy and kissed him. He apologised for being late and they drove off. He was withdrawn at dinner and Jasmine felt uneasy. The pub was noisy and crowded, but it was if they existed apart from it in their own silent capsule. Jasmine chipped away at the ice and told him a little about her fainting episode and the doctor's advice.

'Yeah. Well you'll have to eat more,' he mumbled.

When they returned to the flat, Jasmine asked Andy where the old bomb was.

'Gone to car heaven. The wreckers.'

'Why? Couldn't you have used it as a trade-in?'

'Not mine to trade-in. It belonged to Johnno,' he snapped.

'Oh,' Jasmine said and left it at that. She sensed his mood. He kissed her on the cheek and said, 'See you Saturday,' Then his phone rang and he went inside.

The area around Military Jetty was popular with fishermen and families, picnicking or throwing a line in. Jasmine's grandfather had told her that the jetty was built in 1941 to help in the transport of men and goods to Fort Bribie which was used in World War Two. Few people knew about its history. It was just an old wooden jetty. Blue and yellow hire boats were moored near the beach and there were nearly always pelicans here. It was a little further south from the boat ramp. The pelicans loved to sit on these boats and they decorated them with their poo, the white stuff dribbling over the sides of the little wooden row boats like icing on a cake. Jasmine didn't have to wait long before Christine drove into the car park in the Rescue Service's four wheel drive. She greeted Jasmine and walked to the back of the vehicle.

'He's ready to go. Aren't you Georgie?' Christine said as she hauled the cage out of the back and sat it on the ground. A few eager children came running up to sticky beak.

'Just stand back kids and be quiet. We don't want George to get a big fright. He's been in hospital,' Christine said. She opened the cage door and eased George out. He wobbled a bit, hopped across the grass, flapped his wings and flew off joining a group of his friends in the sky.

'Bye Baby,' Christine said. Jasmine noticed that she was a bit teary. 'Trouble is you get so damned attached to them,' Christine said as she returned the cage.

'Christine I've been meaning to ask you something,' Jasmine said. 'I'd really like to help at the Centre if you'll have me.'

'We are always wanting volunteers,' Christine said. 'When could you come?'

'Well I have most Mondays off, so I could come then. What sort of jobs could I do?'

'To start it won't be very glamorous. Cleaning out cages, feeding the birds, transporting them. But then you might be able to assist in operations or do talks or fund raising.'

'I guess. I could try,' Jasmine replied. Christine thanked her and drove off.

That's what I've always wanted. I want to work with the birds. I could learn so much and then, maybe I could study...maybe.'

Easter Saturday lived up to the Coast's reputation, "Beautiful one day, perfect the next". Jasmine felt so happy for Amanda. She and Megan were going over to Amanda's at twelve o'clock to help her get ready. They would be there to calm her nerves and to fix up any last minute hitches which were common at weddings.

Jasmine sat down in the kitchen with her mum. She started eating her cereal as Susie made toast.

'Did the doctor ring you?' Susie asked.

'Yes Mum.'

'Did she talk about your diet, the psychotherapist?'

'What? Did she ring you too?' Jasmine said angrily. Susie shrugged and looked guilty.

'Mum. This is my business okay. God. I don't need you or any damn doctor fussing about my weight.' She shoved her chair back. 'I wish you'd all fucking leave me alone. I need to get out of this goddamn place,' she screamed. She stormed out the door and down the street. *It makes me so mad. I'll move out. It's about time I had a place of my own. Bloody Mum can be so goddamn protective.*

Amanda walked down the red carpet in her boofy dress. That's what she and Megan called it. But it did look good. Amanda had lost heaps of weight, although her boobs were still big and threatened to pop out of the strapless bodice. The beading around the bust and the waistline was just perfect, the tiny beads sparkling in the April sunshine, matching Amanda's excited face. Her dark shoulder-length hair looked very natural, pulled back gently to the clasp at the back of her head which held the gossamer veil. Jasmine had tears in her eyes as she imagined herself making a lifelong commitment to the man of her dreams. Andy had his arm around her tiny waist and he whispered in her ear. 'One day that will be you. Walking down the aisle. A beautiful princess.' She kissed him and hugged him tighter. He'd scrubbed up pretty well she thought. A smart black shirt and pants that he'd bought especially for the occasion.

Andy drank in Jasmine's perfume. She always smelt inviting, sexy. She'd bought a new dress, midnight blue she called it. It was made of a soft fabric, with narrow shoulder straps, fitted around her neat breasts and falling in layers to just above her knees. He ran his hand over her thigh and thought of making love to her. God it was so good.

'Andy, concentrate,' she giggled. 'I want to hear the vows. Amanda wrote them herself.'

He blew gently in her ear. 'Wait till I get you later.'

ELEVEN

They'd found a table near the front of the pub overlooking the beach. A continuous line of cars droned along the esplanade and busy shoppers streamed past. It was Easter, one of the busiest times on the coast and you could pick the tourists. They ambled, stopped, chatted and looked around a little lost. They had all the time in the world.

Brad sat chatting to his mate Dan. Liam was joining them later.

'Hey Bro, still coming to the Music Festival?' Dan asked, slurring through a mouthful of chips.

'Yep. I bloody well hope so. Jacko better not ring up. Not at Easter or I'll be pissed,' Brad said. They chatted about footy and girlfriends.

'Hey what happened to that Julia bird?' Dan asked.

'She's gone mate. Went back to Sydney.'

'What did you do to her?'

'Not enough obviously,' Brad said. He took a long drink of beer. 'Said I was away on the boat too much or some shit.'

Liam arrived with a towel around his neck and his new girlfriend Kylie attached to his waist.

'Sorry guys. It's the fuckin' traffic. We went for a surf at Alex but just getting here was a bloody nightmare. It's all those touros on the road.'

'Easter mate. That's the problem,' Dan said.

Brad couldn't help looking at Kylie's cleavage. She had boobs straining to pop out of her bikini top. She'd tied a sarong around her waist, but Brad could imagine the rest of the tiny swimsuit hiding under there.

'Brad are you bringing a chick to the Festival? What about Julia?'Liam said.

'Nope. Julia's old news.'

'Hey Kyles, why don't you bring one of your single friends for Brad? They'd think he's so hot,' Liam said digging Brad in the ribs. Kylie half-smiled but looked around bored.

They all headed off to get more drinks and snacks leaving Brad at the table. His thoughts went to Jasmine. He'd ask her, only she was with Andy, the prick. He liked her smile, her sleek body, the way she tucked her hair behind her ear, and how she could fire up. But she wasn't interested... he could tell.

It was an Easter tradition to go to the festival. A group of them were taking off for Caloundra tomorrow. The event was held every Easter, and was very popular, with some top Aussie pop groups performing. He had to go to his mum's first to accompany her to church, but he wasn't going to tell his mates that.

It was Easter Sunday and Brad had kept the promise to his mum. He was sitting beside her in church. *Why am I here? Any normal bloke would be in bed at this hour... or having great sex. I hope I don't see anyone I know.*

Things hadn't changed much since he was a kid, when he'd trailed behind his mum to church every week wearing his Sunday Best and hair slicked back. It was a dull place, light filtering in rainbow colours through the stained glass window above the altar. This was the only thing left from the old days. The old church had been totally refurbished and expanded, so now it looked more like a meeting hall, except for that window. Gone were the plaster figures of Mary and Jesus, the grottos, the confessionals, the communion rails. But guilt still lurked there, guilt for all those sins. Were they mortal or venial? In his mind he saw a little boy in black shorts and white shirt, kneeling, confessing. He was never sure what to confess so he made stuff up. It would be a different story now. He smiled at the thought. He'd be saying the rosary continually for his penance.

He sat low in his seat and glanced around furtively at the rows of serious faces focussed on the priest. Sweat was dribbling down his face and he squirmed in his seat. His mum was wearing one of her old floral dresses. Her hair was pinned back making her angled facial features more severe. Everyone stood, and a motley of voices joined in singing the strains of the hymn "Morning has Broken.'' Cheryl was singing softly and Brad wondered about her. *What is she thinking? What does she dream of? What's she got to look forward to?* She looked so lonely, defeated. She clung to her religion but he wondered how it had helped.

He was glad he came because it meant so much to her. It was the least he could do after all she had done for him. Who was at his bedside when he was in hospital with that broken arm? Who helped him with homework? Who came to all his footy matches and patched him up afterwards? Who was it waiting up late to check that he made it home safely? And she put up with his teenage outbursts and abuse. He'd never forget that.

'Thanks for coming Brad. I really appreciate it,' Cheryl said afterwards.

'That's okay, but I can't see why you keep going. Do you really believe in all that crap?'

'Brad. Of course I do. It's what keeps me going. If I haven't got prayer what have I got?'

'Well, people do other things. There are other religions. You don't always have to go to a church to get spiritual help.'

'I do,' Cheryl said. 'It's all I know Brad.'

After Brad dropped her off, Cheryl drove to the hospital. They were still treating John in the psychiatric ward. He was much improved without access to the grog, although he was dosed up with drugs, mostly anti-depressants. The doctors said he'd be able to come home soon, but he would have to have regular check-ups and be carefully monitored.

She followed the Nambour-Bli Bli Road as it snaked along the edges of the picturesque valley. Most of the cane farms in the valley had gone now due to falling world sugar prices, and the mill in town had closed down. She remembered when they lived in Nambour. The little cane locos rattled right through the centre of town pulling wagons loaded with cut cane to the mill. A huge chimney belched smoke which blanketed the town if there was no wind to take it elsewhere, and steam hissed as you drove down Mill Street. There was always the smell of molasses in the air at cane harvest time, and black soot wafted in from the cane fires like grubby snowflakes coating everything in a black smudge. She often cursed as she rushed out to the clothesline to rescue her clean washing from the black plague.

Every year there was a Sugar Festival after the harvest, a street parade with marching girls and rowdy bands, convoys of vintage cars and colourful floats. Leading the parade was one of the locos festooned with streamers and sugar stalks. Of course there was a Sugar Princess on her throne waving like the queen with a frozen smile. They took Brad when he was little. He perched on John's shoulders and laughed and clapped as the parade made its way down the main street.

Their marriage had endured despite the hardships. It was John's second marriage, his first wife unable to handle his erratic moods. He was permanently scarred by his Vietnam war experiences, physically and mentally. He was caught in crossfire and a bullet had lodged in his hip leaving him with a limp and tormenting memories. After the war he worked on several building sites, but he always argued with the boss or got into fights with other workers, so he set up his own business selling building materials and building cabinets.

Cheryl was a late starter, marrying John when she was 32. She'd had a few relationships in her twenties but she was a restless soul and wanted to live life and travel before settling down. A year after they married, Brad was born, the best day of her life she always reckoned.

She was working as a receptionist at the RSL when she met John. He came to build the cabinets in the club's refurbished kitchen. She was drawn to his smile and sense of humour. Over time she chipped away at his tough exterior and came to know the real John. She believed she could help him, make his life happier. But the demons ate away at him, playing with his mind and terrorising him. There were times when his depression sucked out her soul. But she would not desert him.

Now as she pulled into the hospital car park she felt a deep sense of foreboding. *When is this going to end? What sort of life am I living? Soon Brad will meet a girl and make his own little family.* She wasn't sure whether she could keep up this charade. That's what it felt like. A charade. She fought the tears as she pressed the button on the lift. A young woman in a dressing gown hobbled towards her. She was attached to a drip machine which she wheeled along with her. There was a strong smell of disinfectant and cigarette smoke. She guessed the girl had been outside the front door of the hospital like several others in hospital clothing. She'd seen them every time she visited. They were out there sucking and puffing as if their life depended on it. Just like her. She was one of them. Addicted.

John was sitting in a chair by the bed staring out at the trees. At least he had a scenic view. He turned as she came in.

'Happy Easter,' she said and bent to kiss him on the cheek.

'What? Easter?' he grumbled.

'I see the Easter Bunny has come,' she smiled as she went over and picked up the chocolate egg on his dresser.

'Yeah some woman put it there. She came in talking about Jesus and I told her to piss off.'

'John,' Cheryl shook her head. 'Anyway how are you?'

'I'll be better when I'm out of this crazy place. All they do is ask me questions and give me tablets. Fat lot of good that does.'

'Well you'll be home soon. That'll be good hey?' She glanced around. The room was still very bare but she noticed this time he had magazines and a library book on the movable tray over his bed. She picked up the book. It was a book by one of his favourite crime writers, Lee Child. He loved escaping into those detective stories. The magazines were an assortment, The Bulletin, Wheels and travel journals.

'Who brought these?' Cheryl asked.

'The nurse took me to the library and I picked them. Wasn't much choice there.'

'They have a library?'

'Yeah. But like I said, not much worth a look.'

He looked back out of the window over the tall trees to the town. 'Do you remember when we lived here. In Nambour?'

'Yeah I do.'

'I remember I marched in the Anzac parade with me mates. We were so proud to march with the diggers, to march for the mates who didn't make it back.But you know some bastards jeered us.'

'That happens. They don't know any better.'

He bent his head and whimpered. 'It was all such a waste. We were conned. Bloody conned. I could never justify why we were there. Never.' Cheryl held him as he shuddered, and she cried inside for the broken man who could not be fixed.

TWELVE

Susie got the phone call at work. The clean laundry arrived and she was packing clean towels and sheets on the shelves in the linen room.

'Susie. It's Detective Baker.'

'Yes,' Susie said hesitantly.

'We have some news for you. A man has been charged this afternoon with Doug Bennett's murder. We thought you might like to know.'

'Thank you. Yes. Thanks. Who was it? What happened?'

'We can't say yet, but I doubt if you'd know him. He wasn't from around here, seems he followed Mr Bennett up here.'

'Do you know why?'

'All we can tell you is that it appears they were both involved in the drug trade.'

'We suspected as much. Does this mean we will be left alone now?'

'Certainly. Unless you have other information for us.'

'No. We don't.'

'Mr Bennett's parents can now go ahead with the funeral arrangements, so you can contact them for the details if you want.'

Susie thanked him and ended the call. She held the phone against her chin, deep in thought. She wanted to go to the funeral, so she'd ask for a few days off. It was a chance to go back down south again and catch up with some old friends. She wondered if Jasmine and Stephen would go. She felt they should, he was their father after all. But she was sure she knew what they'd say.

And she was right. Stephen said a very definite NO. A bomb wouldn't move him when he dug his heels in. Jasmine said she'd think about it. When Susie mentioned staying with their good friends Jan and Peter in the Northern Suburbs, she could see Jasmine's mind ticking over. Jasmine was very good friends with Anita, Jan and Peter's daughter. They'd kept in touch over the years and visited a few times.

'You should be able to get a few days off and we could stay for the weekend as well. We could go to the city, do some shopping, go to Watson's Bay like we used to.'

Jasmine shrugged. 'I'm going to my room. I have a painting to finish.'

The plane banked in preparation for its landing at Botany Bay. Susie pressed her face to the window and drank in the postcard setting below, the familiar Opera House sails, the coat hanger bridge, the sparkling harbour dotted with tiny boats, and all those inlets. Sydney really was a water city. She wished she was visiting for cheerier reasons but the good thing was that Jasmine was here beside her. They both just loved Sydney.

The funeral was a sombre and disorganised affair. It seemed to be thrown together at the last minute. There were no photos, no program books. Susie cringed at the songs Doug's parents had picked. They obviously didn't know Doug very well. He didn't have an ounce of the religious in him, so the hymn "The Lord is My Shepherd" just didn't fit. Jasmine and Susie sat close together feeling awkward. Doug's parents sat up the front with his sister Ellen. Doug's father had aged noticeably since they'd last seen him. He was very grey and fragile looking, with a wheel chair close beside him.

Relations with Doug's parents had soured with the divorce. They had wiped Susie and the kids, which was sad Susie thought, because it left Jasmine and Stephen without grandparents. And who knows what Doug had told his parents. They would believe him totally, to them he could do no wrong. She wondered if they'd taken the blinkers off yet, faced reality.

Cindy made a brief appearance then exited before the final prayer. Susie barely recognised some of the relatives. Aunt Sally was in her eighties now and white-haired. There were work colleagues from Doug's earlier business. A couple of them smiled and nodded at her but she felt uncomfortable, hollow inside. *How sad to depart this world like this. Why did he make those choices? It could only end in tragedy. I could have helped him. It wasn't too late.* Susie hung her head and dabbed at her eyes.

Outside the grey skies had opened as if on cue and the mourners dispersed as quickly as they had assembled. There didn't seem to be any gathering afterwards. Not that she was aware of anyhow. People were dashing for their cars or sheltering under umbrellas. Except for one young girl standing by the door.

She would make a statement anywhere. She was a slim girl who looked about early twenties. Her hair was cut pixie short and it was dyed bright orange. She wore a short fitted black dress, black stockings and chunky boots. Susie wondered where she'd come from. Did she lose her accompanying pop band?

Had she taken the wrong directions and ended up at the wrong venue?

She turned as Susie and Jasmine walked out.

'Excuse me,' she said looking at Jasmine. 'Are you Doug's daughter?'

Jasmine nodded. 'Yes.'

She looked at Susie. 'And you must be the ex am I right?'

'I'm Susie,' Susie replied abruptly.

'I'm Petria,' she said. 'I'm Doug's daughter.' Further puzzled looks were exchanged between Jasmine and Susie.

'I'm sorry. You probably don't know about me do you? Dad kept it quiet. My mum is Tracey. I was born before he met and married you...Susan isn't it?'

'Susie. I'm called Susie.'

'So Dad didn't mention me?' Petria continued. Jasmine and Susie shook their heads in unison. 'Well he was funny like that. A man of secrets.'

'Where ... where do you live Petria?'Susie asked. Her voice warbled. She was in a vacuum.

'In the city. I'm an artist and I work with the theatre company. Do their backdrops, some costuming.'

'Did you see Doug...your dad much?' Susie asked frowning.

'Not a lot. But we kept in touch. I knew he had another daughter...and a son is that right?'

'Yes Stephen. He's 15,' Susie said.

'Didn't he come?' Petria asked looking around.

'No. He...,' Susie said.

Petria hugged Jasmine. 'Cool. I know my half-sister at last. How awesome.' Susie and Jasmine were still in shock, unmoving, their faces stiff.

'I'm so sorry to throw this on you. I thought you would know. Anyway it'd be nice to catch up. Here's my number.' She scribbled a number on the back of a card and handed it over. Her phone beeped and she glanced at it. 'There's my lift. I have to go. Bye.' And she was off in a whirlwind dodging puddles as she ran to the car park.

'Did that just happen?' Susie said as they stared after Petria. The two women looked at each other and burst out laughing.

'I wonder how old she is,' Susie said.

'She looks a bit older than me, I think.'

'But what if...what if...'

'Mum. No. She said she was born before you and Doug were married.'

'But it still could have been...you know when I was going out with him. He never said anything.'

'Come on. Let's go.' Jasmine half-dragged her mum back to the rental car. Susie was still muttering.

'I don't understand why he didn't tell me.' Then she stopped and looked pointedly at Jasmine. 'How do we know she's his daughter? She could be making it up.'

'Why? Why would she do that?'

Susie shrugged. 'Money maybe. She might be after some of his money.'

'But she knew stuff, Mum. She knew about me and Stephen.'

'Yeah maybe.' Susie paused. 'It's just weird that's all.'

'Well we could catch up before we go back. That'll give us more info. Besides I want to get to know my sister.' Jasmine smiled.

Jasmine and Susie had taken the Watson's Bay ferry from Circular Quay. The incessant rain of yesterday had retreated leaving a smiling crystal sky. The ripples of water in the harbour were pinpricked with glitters of sunlight as the ferry motored past Fisherman's Island and Rose Bay. The boat docked and disgorged its passengers, most of them flowing towards the fish and chips cafe. It was a tradition to go to Watson's Bay and feast on fish and chips.

They decided to go for a walk first as it was still too early for lunch. They headed up the hill away from the crowds at the restaurant and cafe. Family groups and couples were picnicking or lounging in the park. They followed the walking track to the left as it took them along a narrow path headed straight for the cliffs. It was as if the land was suddenly cut off and fell away to the turbulent ocean metres below. This was the Gap, the sandstone cliffs at the harbour entrance, Sydney's South Head. It was popular with visitors because of its raw beauty and winding walking tracks. It was notorious not only for its danger to shipping, but also as its attraction as a suicide spot. It was calculated that about 50 people a year chose to end their lives by leaping off the cliffs into the angry waters below.

They took their time walking up the ragged path and the steep steps that took them to the peak of the headland. They plonked themselves on a wooden bench right near the lookout. A group of Asian tourists were posing for photos at the railing and they jostled and nattered in their foreign language. Jasmine started texting with her phone. When she was done Susie said, 'Jasmine. I want you to be honest. How are you...really? I mean with all that's been happening.'

'I'm fine,' she said turning her head away. The stiff breeze picked her loose hair up and flicked it all over her face. She brushed it back and pulled a hair tie from her wrist to secure the wayward strands into a ponytail. Susie patted her on the leg.

'I worry about you. That's all.'

'Well don't. You worry about yourself...or Stephen.' She looked down as her phone beeped. Susie treasured these moments with her daughter. She could feel the bond between them weakening and she was finding it hard to deal with. Soon Jasmine would move out and Susie knew how lost she'd feel without her in the house. She dreaded the future when both kids were gone. What then? All she could see now was a deep black chasm of nothingness.

'How's this thing with Andy going?' Susie asked.

'Yeah. Good. I really like him. We have fun together,' Jasmine said.

'You don't bring him home much.'

'Mum. There's nothing in Caloundra. Everyone goes to Mooloolaba.'

'You seem to be the one always going to him that's all.'

'Well Mum. You won't have to worry any more. He's asked me to move in with him.'

'What?' Susie spun around to face her.

'He just sent a text. He's moving out of that dodgy flat he shares with Brad.'

'Where's he moving to?' Susie was getting more anxious by the second.

'Still in Mooloolaba. But it's a jazzy new unit on the beachfront. I can't wait.'

Susie sat back in the seat and sighed. 'This is very sudden.'

'No it isn't. I've been talking about moving out for ages.'

'I meant moving in with Andy. You really haven't known him that long.'

'Long enough. It'll be perfect,' Jasmine said as she tucked loose strands of hair behind her ear. Jasmine started texting again and Susie stood up and went over to the lookout railing. The relentless waves smashed onto the rocks far below just like the pounding in her own heart. She cried silent tears. She knew Jasmine would move out eventually, and it was good for her to be independent. But somehow she felt deflated, abandoned. She always remembered the saying, "A mother holds her children's hands for a little while, their hearts forever." How true that was.

Before they flew back to Queensland, Jasmine and Susie met Petria for lunch at Circular Quay. She was so pleased to see them. As she spoke, her eyes ablaze and her hands and arms in constant motion, Susie thought how different she was from Jasmine in personality. If Petria was indeed Jasmine's sister, Susie could see few resemblances except for the artistic streak. Petria told them she was nearly 25 and that she had seen little of Doug since she was very young. He'd often taken her and her mum to the beach in those early years. Susie made a mental calculation and felt relieved that Petria was born before she and Doug got together. But then Susie asked if Petria had any early photos.

'As a matter of fact I have,' Petria said delving into her bag. She pulled out three photos, two were of herself as a baby and toddler, and the third was a photo of Petria at about three sitting with her mum and Doug at the beach. An all smiling happy family. It was dated on the back "1987". Susie's mouth fell open and a chill ran down her spine. She and Doug were together then, they married that year. The truth hit her like a lightning bolt. He had a secret family on the side. *The bastard. Why didn't he tell me? How could I have been so blind?* Maybe there was some mistake. He wouldn't do that.

'Mum. What is it?' Jasmine asked.

'Nothing,' Susie swallowed. 'It's just a shock you know.'

'Do you think Jasmine and I looked alike as little kids?' Petria asked.

'Yes. There is a likeness,' Susie said. They certainly had the same eyes, those deep set eyes, just like Doug's.

If meeting Petria was a shock, then another surprise was waiting for Susie when she arrived home. Stephen told her that Doug's solicitor had called and wanted her to call back as soon as possible. Stephen had survived well enough in their absence, and judging by the overflowing bin spilling out takeaway boxes, he had provided the takeaway places with plenty of his custom. He actually seemed to have missed his mum, chatting and conversing amicably with her.

The solicitor told Susie that Jasmine and Stephen were beneficiaries of Doug's estate along with Petria who had a third share as well. He couldn't elaborate on the details at this stage he said.

'Well,' Susie said. 'You guys are lucky. I wonder how much money we're talking here. Can I maybe get a loan?' she joked.

'I'll think about it,' Stephen quipped. Susie sent Jasmine a text and got a message back. "Don't get 2 excited Mum. He was probably in debt up to his eyeballs."

THIRTEEN

The view from the balcony was spectacular. The unit was on the tenth floor and it looked right over Mooloolaba Beach to the rolling waves of the turquoise Pacific. To the right was Point Cartwright with its lofty lighthouse and million dollar properties. A bright yellow pilot boat had just emerged from the harbour canal on its way to guide a huge ship into the Brisbane shipping lanes. To the left the sandy beaches stretched as far as Coolum in the misty haze.

Andy lounged on the deck chair and puffed on his cigarette. *This is the life mate. I'm so happy to be away from that dodgy flat and Brad hassling me all the time. It's so good to have money at last.* His phone beeped but it wasn't Jasmine this time. He knew she was flying home this afternoon so he was expecting her any minute. The message was from Johnno. Again. He said the cops were on his case. They'd searched his house last night. He wondered how they'd tracked Johnno down.

They'd been careful to cover their tracks. And Johnno was way up in the mines. Dysart for fuck sake.He'd have to be careful. This murder, now bloody Johnno. What next?

There was a soft tapping at the door. Jasmine. He swept her off her feet and swung her around.

'Babe. Welcome to your new home.' He smothered her in kisses. Then he ushered her to the balcony and swept his arm over the view like a hostess on a game show sweeping her arms over the prizes.

'Voila my sweet. What do you think?'

'Wow Andy. It's so cool. I'll feel like I'm in a palace. A princess in a palace.'

'That's it. And now to christen the unit.' He picked her up again while she giggled and struggled.

'Andy. Put me down. I just got here.' He carried her through to the bedroom and plonked her on the bed quickly undressing, and then jumping on top of her, peeling her layers off, madly kissing her all over.

'God I missed you Babe. You have no idea,' he puffed and groaned. They clung together and rolled several times nearly falling off the edge of the bed.

'Andy,' Jasmine gasped. But he'd waited too long. He wanted her, he needed to possess her, to let go of all of his stresses. He entered her and became overwhelmed in a world of ecstasy. Jasmine groaned and tried to go with him.

'I missed you too,' she whispered.

It was all over too quickly but Andy was in heaven. He sat up and reached for his smokes. His phone beeped but he ignored it this time.

'I can't believe it,' Andy said inhaling the smoke. 'I'm in this really cool place with a hot chick in my bed. Man it can't get any better.' Jasmine propped herself up on one elbow.

'You haven't asked me about my trip yet?'

'Oh sorry Babe,' Andy said putting his cigarette on the ashtray. He grabbed at her again.

'Well how was it?'

'So much happened. I don't know where to start. But the big news is I have a sister in Sydney I didn't know about.'

'How come?'

'Seems like she was born before Mum and Doug got together. He was with another woman, Tracey. He never told us about it. Petria...that's her name, she's interesting, an arty type.' Jasmine sat up , put her t-shirt back on and flicked her hair back.

'What did Brad think about you moving out?' Jasmine asked.

'He doesn't know.'

'What? Why?'

'He's still out on the trawler. I left a note.'

'Do you think he'll get someone else in?'

'Who knows? Who cares?' He moved in to grab her again.

'What about that Johnno guy, the one with the old wrecked car?'

'What about him?' Andy snapped.

'Well didn't he stay there?'

'Who said that? I never said he was there.' He sat up angrily and pulled his shorts on. Jasmine finished getting dressed as Andy walked off to the bathroom.

'Sorry I asked,' she muttered under her breath. Why did he turn so jumpy and defensive? The mention of Johnno hit a nerve.

There was a knock at the door. Jasmine couldn't believe it. There in front of her were two detectives showing their badges. It was as if the police were tracking her. She recognised Detective Baker but not the other man, a short efficient looking man with a moustache.

'Well hello again, Jasmine,' Detective Baker said. 'I didn't expect to see you here. This is Detective Summers. We have a search warrant for the premises. Is Andrew Pascoe here?' Jasmine turned as Andy walked from the hallway towards her adjusting his shorts.

'What's going on?' he demanded. The men explained why they were there.

'What are you after? I only just moved in here.' His face was going red and he ran his hand through his messed-up hair.

'We can't tell you, except that we have received information which requires us to search the premises.'

Andy shrugged. 'Do what you have to do.' He opened the door wider and the men moved in.

They made their way down the hall first, pulling gloves on as they walked. Jasmine frowned at Andy then went out to the balcony with him.

'Andy what are they after? What have you done?' she whispered urgently.

'Nothing. I swear. I just moved in. Maybe it was the people in here before us. Fucked if I know.'

The men came out into the living area, going through kitchen cupboards, upturning cushions, checking light fittings. They spotted Jasmine's backpack and shoulder bag.

'We'll need to check those too,' Baker said.

'But I just flew in from Sydney. I've never set foot in this place before,' Jasmine said. They unzipped her backpack, pulling out scrunched up dirty clothes. *How embarrassing.* A lip gloss fell and rolled across the floor. They shoved it all back. The short man with the moustache was prying in her shoulder bag. *Nothing's private.* Then she froze, her mouth dropped open. The detective was smirking and holding up three small plastic bags of white powder, bags just like the one she found near the park. Jasmine looked over at Andy. He coughed and turned his face away.

'Now Miss,' Detective Summers said, 'would you mind explaining why you have these.'

'I...I,' Jasmine spluttered. 'They are not mine. I never put them there.'

'Well who did then?' he asked. Jasmine looked at Andy for support but he just shrugged.

'I don't know. God.' Jasmine started to cry. 'They weren't there before.' The detectives told her to sit down. Andy brought her some water. The detectives addressed Andy.

'What do you know about this?'

Andy grimaced. 'Jasmine just got here. Maybe someone planted it, someone in Sydney, someone on the plane.'

Jasmine was shaking her head. 'No. No. No. Those bags weren't there in Sydney or on the plane. I know. I went to the toilet when we arrived back at Maroochydore. I reefed around in my bag for the lip gloss. I know there were no bags there then.' The policemen looked at Andy.

'Did you put them in her bag?' Detective Summers said.

'Shit. No. Why would I do that? I'm no drug lord.'

'We didn't say you were. Those bags got there somehow and we will find out.'

They told Jasmine and Andy that they would both have to come to the station to make statements as soon as the bags' contents were tested and verified.

'Let's hope for your sake Jasmine that it's nothing sinister,' Baker said and raised his eyebrows.

After they left, Jasmine rolled into a ball on the couch and burst into tears. *This can't be happening. Why me? I didn't do anything. Someone put that stuff there.*

She jumped up, her face wet and mucus coming from her nose.

'Did you put it there?' she screamed at Andy. He'd never seen her like this before. She was like a madwoman.

'No,' he yelled. 'Why the fuck would I do that? I don't do that stuff. It must've been someone at the airport. Someone got hot feet and stashed it there or something.'

'It's not fair,' Jasmine sobbed. 'It's not fuckin' fair.'

Andy wrapped his arms around her, sat her down, kissed her head.

'It's okay. We'll sort it. They'll find out it wasn't you.'

Jasmine cried even louder.

It was the next day, Monday, and Jasmine found herself back at the police station. They'd called her in first. Andy was to come later. They had identified the substance as cocaine. The procedures were much the same as her previous interviews, but this time they focussed on her and Andy. She had to tell them when they met, where they met, who his friends were, where they went.

'Why are you asking me all this? What's Andy got to do with it?'

'We are following up on leads linked to your father Doug Bennett's murder. He was heavily involved in the drug trade and there were links here on the coast. Obviously one person has been arrested, but as you know, several people are involved in these drug rings. We need as much information as you can give us,' Detective Baker said.

'I still don't understand why you think he's involved.'

'You told us about a car you saw that night, the night of the alleged drug exchange, a car with a distinctive boot.'

'That's right.'

'We managed to track it down and we located the owner.'

'I think it may have been a guy called Johnno.'

'Who is this Johnno?' the detective asked.

'I don't know, but I know that a car like that old car belonged to him. Only it mightn't be the same car. I'm not sure.'

'How did you come by this information?'

Jasmine told them how she'd asked about the old bomb parked in the driveway at the flat, and was told it belonged to a guy called Johnno.'

'So the car was parked at your boyfriend's flat?'

'Yes.'

'Did Andy ever drive it?'

'I don't know. Why?'

'Why didn't you tell us you recognised it as the same one that you saw at Caloundra?'

'I didn't take much notice of it at first. It was out in the dark. I really only noticed the strange boot a week or so ago, and then I wasn't sure. After that it disappeared.'

'Did you ever notice any drug activity at that flat?'

'No. Andy smoked pot every now and then. But that's all.'

'Any strange phone calls, visitors, any suspicious activity while you were there?'

'No. Nothing.' Jasmine was feeling increasingly uneasy. *What about Andy's continuous phone calls, his frequent meetings, his jumpy behaviour, his sudden wealth?* She pushed the thoughts to the back of her head.

'Did you ever wonder why your friend Andy could afford an expensive car, and an up market unit?'

'He said his parents helped him. There's nothing wrong with that is there?'

'Not if you have rich and generous parents,' Detective Baker smiled wryly. He shifted forward in his chair and looked Jasmine right in the eye. 'Look. You have already been implicated with that money in the boot of your car. Why don't you come clean with us and we'll go more lightly on you.'

'I told you. I don't do drugs. There is no reason to think I'm involved. I did not know those drugs were there.'

'You were there with him. Andy is your boyfriend. I think that is a good reason.'

Jasmine shook her head and sobbed.

'We will have to charge you with possession of a dangerous drug. And there is a lot of it, so that suggests it was to be used in trafficking. You will be required to go before a magistrate in court.'

Jasmine's face was drained of colour. *Court? Magistrate? I'm innocent. God I'm going to be sick.* She jumped up holding her mouth. 'I need a bathroom. Quick.'

Jasmine walked out of there in a numbed state. *What do I do now?* Andy would be on his way to the station and she didn't feel like going back to that unit. It would be like a tomb. She'd drive to Caloundra and pack some of her things. That would keep her busy. Her mum would be at work so she'd have the place to herself. No probing questions. She couldn't tell her yet. She'd totally freak out.

On the way out of town she decided to go by Brad's flat. Part of her wanted to see him. Maybe he would understand. She'd see if he was home. She'd left her denim jacket in the lounge room last time she was there. It was a good excuse anyway.

As she pulled up she saw Brad's ute in the driveway. But he could still be on the trawler because he often got a lift with his mate. She thought she'd try anyway, so she tapped on the door and pushed. It was open.

'Brad,' she called, peering in.

A young waif-like girl came out of the bedroom wearing a large men's t-shirt which fell in folds around her thin body. Her hair was a tangled mess. *God she looks about sixteen.*

'Hi,' she said, 'Brad'll be out soon.' The girl went to the fridge and grabbed a cola, ripped the top off and flopped on the sofa.

'Jasmine, hi,' Brad said as he came down the hall looking guilty. 'If you're after Andy I'm afraid he's done a runner.'

'No. I know where Andy is. I've just come for my jacket. I left it here in the lounge room somewhere.' She started scanning the room. She found it on the floor near the TV. ' Thanks.' She backed towards the door. 'Sorry to intrude.' She scampered down the stairs but Brad was close behind.

'Jasmine. Wait. What's wrong? You look like you've seen a ghost.'

Jasmine stopped but she couldn't face him. She started to cry and bit her lip. Brad walked over closer.

'Jaz. What is it?'

She shook her head and opened the car door. 'You wouldn't want to know,' she said.

'What has that fuckwit Andy done now?' Brad said.

'Nothing. It's nothing,' Jasmine said as she wiped her face, closed the door roughly and drove off.

Why was everything going so wrong? First Andy. I really like what we had, but could I trust him now? And Brad. How could he sleep with such a young chick? But it is none of my business. Why should I care?

She drove south through a veil of tears. There was no one she could turn to. Amanda was still on her honeymoon and Megan just wouldn't understand. It all seemed so hopeless.

When she arrived home, she threw some washing in the machine and packed some clean clothes in a suitcase. But it was all so mechanical. Where was she going? She didn't feel like going with Andy now. Her mother would just say, 'See what happens? You didn't think it out.' Brad would say, 'I told you so.' She just wanted it all to go away. The tears flowed freely and sobs racked her body.

She went into her mother's room and opened the top drawer of the bedside cabinet. The painkillers her mum used for migraine were looking up at her, enticing her. She popped the seals of the first sheet of tablets and threw a handful into her mouth. She rushed to the kitchen and swallowed a full glass of water to wash them down. Head down, she scuffed off to her room, curled up on the bed and closed her heavy eyes.

FOURTEEN

He felt so guilty. Why did he drink so much, let himself lose control? *This is not me. It is not who I am.*

Brad looked at his face in the mirror. He'd just returned from a week at sea and a wild man peered back at him. His dark curly hair was sticking out at odd angles. The drinking session last night had left its scars under his eyes and his tongue was swollen and furry. He washed his face and shook his head. Ouch. Someone was using a jackhammer in there.

The young girl Nicole had gone home. Nick was still holed up in the second bedroom with his chick. *What the fuck was I thinking? Those two chicks only looked about sixteen, but they knew how to play the game.* It was hot sex, but somehow instead of feeling great, he felt disappointed. Why did he give in?

And then Jasmine had to turn up. He could have explained to her, apologised, but what for? This was his business. Why did it rattle him so much? He was worried about her. Who knows what Andy had done. Andy didn't deserve her. He wanted to call her but he didn't have her number. He could ask Andy but that wouldn't go over too well. Then he had an idea. He'd send Andy a message asking for the number and telling him that he wanted to tell her about the jacket she'd left at the flat. It was worth a try anyway.

No message or call came back. Just when he'd almost given up, he got Andy's message saying he'd come around himself to pick the jacket up. *Shit. That didn't work.* Andy called around soon after and barged in the door.

'Yeah. Where's the jacket?' His face was flushed and he smelt of pot.

'You're too late. She picked it up herself,' Brad said.

'How long ago? You should have called me. Where is she now?'

'It wasn't long ago. She didn't say where she was going.'

Andy rushed off down the stairs. Brad followed him.

'What happened Andy?'

He turned around, his eyes ablaze. 'What da ya mean?'

'Jasmine looked upset. What happened?'

'How the fuck should I know? Mind your own fuckin' business.'

He jumped in the car and started it up. The window was down so Brad yelled, 'You owe money for the electricity.' Andy reversed out and spun off giving Brad the rude finger gesture.

Brad took some painkillers, hoping that would help his head, and stretched out on the couch. A blade of light was slicing through the curtains right into his eyes. He got up and pulled the curtains shut. He felt like a monster wave had hit him.

But he couldn't stop thinking about Jasmine. Something was going on. How could he get her number? Andy wouldn't give it and he didn't know any of her friends or family. He knew she worked at the zoo but they wouldn't give out numbers. She talked about pelicans a lot and how she wanted to save the ones in trouble, and he remembered Andy had mentioned visiting the Bird Rescue Service. After he'd found the number in the white pages on his iphone, he called the Rescue Service and spoke to Christine.

'Yes,' she said. 'I know Jasmine. She just loves her pelicans. She was supposed to come in today so I'm not sure what happened. I'm sure she'll call later.' She gave Brad the number. 'If you get onto her, tell her I'm right for today now. Maybe she can come next Monday.'

Jasmine's phone rang out every time he called. He didn't want to leave a message. Andy might have access to her phone and wonder what's going on. He didn't want to make problems for her. There was nothing he could do for now, so he curled up and dozed off.

He was woken up a few hours later by loud knocking at the door. Bleary-eyed and yawning he staggered to the door. Two officious looking men in suits showed their badges.

'I'm Detective Baker and this is Detective Summers. We believe Andrew Pascoe resided here.'

'Yes. But he's moved out.'

'Yes we know where he lives. Would you be the flatmate Bradley Nash?'

'Yes. I'm Brad,' Brad said frowning, his mind ticking over. *What's up? Speeding? Drinking? The young girls? No they asked about Andy.*

'Could we come in? We have a few questions. You might be able to give us more information about Andrew Pascoe,' Detective Baker said.

'Yeah. Sure.' Brad ushered them in, moving some dirty clothes off the couch so they could sit. He sat opposite in the broken chair. A loose spring dug into his bum so he grabbed a cushion to cover it.

'How long have you lived here?' Baker asked. The shorter moustached detective was taking notes.

'About two years or close to,' Brad said.

'And Andrew how long was he here?'

'About the same time. We took out the lease together.'

'Did any other people live here during that time?'

'No. Not really,' Brad said. 'A few people crashed here after parties but they didn't live here. There was Andy's mate Johnno. He stayed for a bit but he left to work in the mines at Dysart.'

'Did anyone here own a dark blue Datsun with a lighter coloured boot?'

'Yes. That was Johnno's.'

'Do you know his surname?'

Brad shook his head looking puzzled. 'It started with a B. Baker, Bates, no Baxter I think.'

'Did he take the car with him?'Baker asked.

'No he left it here. It wasn't very reliable.'

'Did anyone else drive it?'

'Andy did sometimes because he didn't have his own car, but it was a bomb. It often broke down.'

'We have reason to believe that a vehicle fitting this description was involved in drug activity. Do you know anything about that?'

Brad shrugged and shook his head.

Baker continued, 'Did you ever see anything suspicious in Andy's behaviour, his friends, his phone calls?'

'I kept out of his way. I work on a trawler. I'm away for a week at a time.'

'But there must have been something.'

'He smoked pot. I had an idea he was involved in something but I kept out of it. Not my business.'

'What about his girlfriend Jasmine?'

'No. Not her. She wouldn't touch the stuff.'

Detective Baker shifted in his seat. 'How do you know?'

'I spoke to her a few times. I know she's a decent chick. I warned her about Andy.'

'How did she react to that?'

'She ignored me. Told me off,' Brad said. Both detectives smiled.

They asked Brad when he saw Andy and Jasmine last and how they were behaving. He told them about Andy's rushed visit and Jasmine's distressed state.

'I've tried to call Jasmine. She was very upset,' Brad said.

'Well she had reason to be upset,' Detective Baker said. Both detectives stood and thanked Brad.

Reason to be upset? What did they mean? What the hell was going on?

After the detectives had left, Brad called Andy.

'What the fuck's going on? The cops were here asking questions,' Brad said.

'What did they want?' Andy growled.

'You tell me. What the hell have you done?'

'Fuck off,' Andy yelled and cut off the call.

FIFTEEN

The school bus had just deposited Stephen near the park. It was only a short walk home but he took his time. He'd just started term two of his year level 10 and already the assignments were being outlined and detailed thick and fast. The holidays weren't long enough. Bloody school work. It sucked. Maybe with a bit of luck his father's payout would be substantial and he could leave school this year. He'd have so many more options with shitloads of money in his pocket.

Jasmine's car was in the driveway. *Wasn't she moving in with that Andy guy? She's probably down at the park drawing pelicans or some shit.*

He dropped his bag at the door and went straight to the fridge. He stood there for a while hoping something good to eat would materialise. Nothing there. He did the same with the pantry. He grabbed a couple of muesli bars and a small packet of chips. His mum often bought those big bags which contained twelve small individual packs. They didn't last long.

He ripped the wrapper off the muesli bar and started munching, then grabbed his bag and slouched off down the hall. Jasmine's door was open so he glanced in. He stopped in surprise. She was on the bed asleep, but something didn't look right. It was the way her head and arm drooped over the edge of the bed.

'Jaz,' he said dropping his bag and food. 'Jaz,' he said again more urgently. He rushed over and shook her, thinking that at any minute she'd tell him to piss off.

But her head flopped back on the pillow. She wouldn't wake up. Stephen started to panic and shake. His mind raced. *DRABC. First aid, danger, response, airways, breathing, circulation.* He could see she was still breathing. *Ambulance. I have to call an ambulance.*

He grabbed his mobile and hit the triple zero buttons. The operators went over the first aid procedures and told him to put Jasmine in the recovery position. The paramedics were on their way. Then he rang Susie.

'Mum. Come quick. Something's wrong with Jaz,' he spluttered.

'What? What happened?'

Stephen told Susie how he'd found her and how the ambulance was coming.

'I'll be there soon.'

By the time Susie screeched to a halt outside their little home, the paramedics had arrived and were treating Jasmine. They had a mask over her face and had just secured her on the stretcher.

Susie raced in. 'Jaz. God. Jaz,' she screamed. She bent over the stretcher and looked up at the paramedics with wide eyes.

'What's wrong with her? What's happened?'

'We're not sure,' the male paramedic said. 'She's unconscious but she has circulation and breathing. We need to get her to hospital.'

As they wheeled her out they fired rapid questions at Susie. 'Has this happened before? Has she any medical conditions? Diabetes? Epilepsy?'

Susie sobbed and shook her head. They offered to take her with them to the hospital but she said she'd follow in her car. She raced back inside to grab some tissues from her bedroom. Then she saw the empty blister sheet from her painkiller pack on the floor. She ripped the drawer open, the rest of the pack was still there. Like a mad woman she ran out screaming at the paramedics who had just shut the doors. She shoved the blister sheet through the window. 'She must have taken these,' she panted. The paramedics took the sheet and nodded as they drove off.

Stephen was standing at the front door frozen and pasty white. Susie was shaking. 'I'll call you Stephen,' she said as she jumped in the car and sped off.

Susie drove like a stunned robot. The hospital was only minutes away and she had driven these streets many times so it was all mechanical. *How long had she been like that? Why did she take those pills? It's all my fault. I should have taken more notice of her stressed state. Poor Jaz. Please God help my little girl. Help her to be okay.*

They had Jasmine in the emergency ward and they were pumping her stomach. A young Indian doctor approached Susie. 'You are Jasmine's mother?'

Susie nodded. 'I'm Susie.' She held a ball of tissues to her mouth.

'She appears to have taken an overdose of painkillers. Would you know when she might have done this?'

Susie shook her head. Her whole body had gone cold. 'I was at work. My son Stephen found her when he came home from school. We didn't even think she'd be home.'

'We are using a stomach pump. The success will depend on how long she's had the drugs in her system.'

Susie sobbed. 'Is she going to be okay?'

'We'll do our best Susie. Hopefully that's all she's taken. You can go over shortly. Just let them finish with the pump and the drip. I'm sure it'll be fine.' The doctor patted her arm and walked off to join the others.

After a short while the Indian doctor waved her over.

'She's waking up. Just don't tire her too much okay.' The medical team moved away except for a nurse checking on the drip.

Susie bent over her daughter. 'Jaz. Jaz. I'm here. It's okay.' The nurse said it was alright to move the mask for a bit.

'Mum,' Jasmine whispered. 'I'm sorry.' She closed her eyes then opened them slowly. 'I feel so tired,' she croaked.

'It's alright. You're going to be fine. I'll be here.' Susie squeezed Jasmine's hand.

'I didn't do it Mum. I can't go to court.'

'Don't worry now. You just rest,' Susie said. *What was she talking about? Court?*

'I'm just popping out so I can let Stephen know you're fine. I'll be back soon.' She replaced the mask and slipped out into the foyer. She rang Stephen and told him the good news, then she said, 'Stephen can you find Jaz's phone and find out Andy's number? I want to call him too.'

Stephen found Jasmine's phone and scrolled through the names. He gave Susie the number.

Susie was filled with trepidation. *What was going on? She was so happy about moving in with Andy. Did he and Jasmine split? Is that why she was so distressed? What was the stuff about a court?*

'Andy. It's Susie. Jasmine's mum.'

'Hello.'

'I thought you might like to know. Jasmine is in hospital.'

'Why? What happened? Is she okay?'

'She's going to be fine. She was distressed and came home. She took too many painkillers.'

'God. That's bad.'

'Andy. What happened ? She was fine when she dropped me off after the airport. Have you guys split?'

'No. No.' He paused. 'There was a raid and the cops found drugs in her bag.'

'God. No. How did they get there? She doesn't do drugs.'

'We had to go to the police station and make statements. I don't know what happened after that. She wouldn't answer her phone.'

'Well I'll talk to her more when she's a bit more awake. They're keeping her in overnight.'

'Yeah well I'll call her later.' And with that he hung up.

Susie never really liked Andy. *There was something about him. Wouldn't you think he'd be rushing down to be at her side? Ever since Jasmine had met him there'd been trouble. And she was always the one running after him. She seemed so blind to it all.*

When she went back inside Jasmine was propped up a bit higher on her pillow and looking around.

'Look at you girl. You are starting to look better already,' Susie said. Jasmine attempted a smile.

'Mum. I feel so silly. I shouldn't be here. In hospital. I would have been okay. I was just having a deep sleep that's all.'

'Stephen did the right thing. You were unconscious.'

Jasmine rolled her eyes and sighed.

'Jaz. Tell me. Why did you come home? You were moving in with Andy.'

'I needed to pack stuff.'

'Tell me about the drug raid,' Susie said. Jasmine turned quickly with fire in her eyes.

'How do you know about that?' she said in a hoarse whisper.

'Andy told me.'

'What? You rang Andy? That's none of your business.' She pouted and flopped her head back on the pillow.

'Well I think it is my business when you nearly kill yourself.'

'God. Don't be so dramatic mum.' She shuffled under the covers. 'I need some sleep.'

Jasmine kept going over what happened. She really liked Andy but why wasn't he here if he knew about it? She kept mentally retracing her steps after the airport toilet visit, to work out whether anyone had the opportunity to slip those drugs into her bag. But it all came back to Andy. How could he do such a thing? She couldn't trust him now.

The doctors said she should have a few days off work to recover fully. They warned her about taking too many painkillers. The danger they said was not in dying, but long term liver damage could result. She decided she'd visit the Rescue Service on her days off. That would keep her mind busy. She rang Christine and arranged to come out.

'Did that old friend of yours reach you?' Christine asked.

'Who?'

'A guy rang and wanted your number. Said he was an old friend and he wanted to contact you. Brad his name was.'

'Brad. Really? I wonder how he knew I was involved with this place?' She paused. 'Did he leave his number?'

'Actually he did.' She gave Jasmine the number. Then Jasmine remembered the missed calls on her phone. She had ignored them because she didn't recognise the number. *Brad. Why was he calling? Why was he going to all that trouble to contact me? I can't talk to him. He'd only say that he'd warned me. Probably act smart-arse about it. And then he slept with that young chick. No he can wait. I need to think this out.*

It was a good decision, Jasmine realised, to come here and spend time with the pelicans. Christine introduced her to the residents of the lake. 'This here is Percy,' she said as she patted the head of a very inquisitive old male who waddled towards them. Following behind him was a smaller female called Polly. 'Those two preening themselves are called Paulie and Pat. And over there,' she said pointing to a lone bird paddling leisurely on the mirrored waters of the lake, 'is another little lady called Pammie.'

'All Ps,' said Jasmine, 'Does that get confusing?'

'Not really,' Christine said. 'Did you ever read the book "Storm Boy"?'

'Yes. I loved it.'

'Well the pelicans in it were all Ps, Mr Percival, Mr Ponder and Mr Proud. I loved that idea.'

'It was a sad story. I cried at the end.'

'You might find working here a bit sad. They're not all success stories you know.'

'Do you know Mr Percival is still alive? He's 33 years old and lives at the Adelaide Zoo. They say he's their best breeder,' Jasmine said. 'So when he dies his memory will live on in his offspring. Just like they said in the story. Birds like him never really die.'

Jasmine cleaned out some cages and fed fish to the pelicans. She met Phil, one of the volunteers, who told her about how recently he brought in several mutton birds that were discovered stranded on the beach. Some of them were close to death. They were able to hand feed three of them and bring them back to health, but sadly the rest died. The local vets donated their time to help out, and autopsies found that the birds had died of starvation and exhaustion. These birds migrated over 150,000 kilometres to reach Australia and they often ran into wild weather. Their journey was a marathon.

After an interesting day tending to the birds, Jasmine headed to the car park and checked her phone again. More missed calls and texts from Andy. She wasn't ready yet.

Even when her mother greeted her when she arrived home, the message was the same. Andy had called around wanting to speak to her. She felt like he was stalking her.

'Did you tell him where I was?'

'No. I didn't think you'd want that. He'll have to wait till you're ready to speak to him.'

Jasmine went to her room, sat on the edge of her bed and chewed her lip. She should call Brad. She felt she owed it to him after his efforts to contact her. Very enterprising she thought. But that other chick he slept with. That annoyed her a bit. Was that what he was really like? She picked up her phone.

'Brad,' she said quietly.

'Hi. Is that you Jaz? Are you okay?'

'Yeah. Good now. Christine at Bird Rescue said you were trying to contact me.'

'I was worried. You looked so upset when you came around the other day.'

'Yes...I...I wasn't thinking too straight.'

'Did something happen with you and Andy?'

'You could say that. But Brad I don't want to talk about it right now.'

'That's fine.' He paused. 'I still want you to come fishing.'

'Yeah. I will. I'm just a bit confused that's all.'

'I'm off on the trawler again, so I'll call when I get back.'

'Thanks Brad,' she said, so quietly he could hardly hear her. She ended the call.

Brad sat looking at the phone for a while. There was something special about Jasmine and he wanted to get to know her better. Protect her. He still wasn't sure what Andy had done, but he knew it couldn't be good. The cops seemed to be on his case so it was inevitable that he would get caught. But what lies had he told Jasmine? Some of those guys were so good at deceit and they learned quickly how to cover their tracks.

SIXTEEN

It was Wednesday afternoon and Andy had been waiting outside Jasmine's house for over two hours. He'd finished work early and he knew she was staying home recovering from her overdose. She wouldn't answer his calls, refused to talk to him. Her car was not there but he assumed she'd come home soon. He was prepared to wait. He didn't want to lose her. He'd had girlfriends before, but none like Jasmine. He really stuffed up this time and he wasn't sure how he'd get out of it.

He felt finally things were happening for him. The job, the money, his girlfriend...now all that was in jeopardy. Where did it all go wrong? He thought he was safe. Johnno said there'd be no problems and he'd trusted him.

While he watched the sun dip behind the Glasshouse Mountains, his thoughts went back to his early days. The pain of his mother's death was etched in his heart forever. It turned their world upside down and back-to-front. It shattered his father and

178

he went into a deep depression. Andy was fourteen and the oldest so it was left to him to look after Aidan and Lachlan because they were still in primary school. He had to grow up overnight, take on responsibility he wasn't prepared for. His father gradually healed, but Andy felt robbed of his teen years. That's when he started smoking pot. At first it was an escape, but then it grabbed him around the throat and wouldn't let go.

He finally made friends with Johnno and Brad, members of the same football team. They trained and played in the local competition. They all followed the Brisbane Broncos team and sometimes travelled to Brisbane to see matches at Suncorp Stadium. Most of the time though, they'd gather at the club, watching their team on the big screen, yelling and cheering, beers glued to their hands.

Andy felt that the problems started when he saw Brad getting good money on the trawlers, working a second job at the Fisheries and sporting a brand new ute and a gorgeous girl friend. Andy wanted that too. Brad seemed so sure of himself but so judgemental. He gave Andy a hard time about his pot smoking, his lack of work and his arrogant attitude.

When Johnno offered him the opportunity to make quick bucks on the side, he jumped at the chance. After all what harm would it do? He could be like Brad, have a new car and a sexy woman. He went for the zoo job even though it was low-paying. It would be a good cover Johnno said. And he'd found Jasmine and that was a really good thing.

He sat up straight when Jasmine's little green Honda eased into the driveway. He jumped out before she had a chance to run inside.

'Just hear me out,' he said. She stopped and faced him.

'You didn't need this shit. I'm sorry.'

'Is that it? Is that all you have to say?'

'Come back. I've been a dickhead.' She glared at him.

'Tell me this, did you put those drugs in my bag?'

'Why would I do that?'

'I don't know what to think right now.'

'Come back. We'll talk about it.'

'What good is talk? It's obvious you're involved in drugs Andy and I don't want a part in it.' She turned to go but Andy grabbed her arm.

'It's not what you think.'

'Let me go,' Jasmine snarled and ran off up the stairs.

'It wasn't me. IT WASN'T FUCKIN'ME !'

Andy staggered back to his car. His head was ready to burst and tears pricked at his eyes. He jumped into his car and banged his fists on the steering wheel. *The bitch. The bitch. No one listens to me. Why is everyone against me?* He revved the car and took off in a shower of gravel. He turned his heavy rock music up full volume and drove like someone demented.

She's no angel. It was her arsehole father. He deserved what he got. And why all the questions about the bomb car? What had she told the cops? I can't even trust her. She probably dobbed me in.

But they'll all pay. Just wait. They'll pay.

Jasmine slammed the door and leaned back on it, her eyes wide.

'What the hell was that?' Susie said as she peered out of the front window.

'He's stalking me.' Jasmine walked over to the table, dropped her bag and sank into a chair. 'He just doesn't get it.'

Stephen sauntered in from his room, his hand dipping into a bag of chips.

'Has that loser left yet?' he said as he munched, and joined Susie at the window.

'What?' Jasmine said.

'That guy. He's been sitting out there for hours. He was there yesterday too.'

'Well he's gone now and I hope he got the message.' Then she spoke softly. 'I should have listened to Brad.'

'Who's Brad?' Stephen asked.

'Oh he's...he lived with Andy, in that flat.' The room stood still for a moment.

'Never mind,' Susie burst out. 'How about we all go out and have fish and chips on the beach. I have some news.' Jasmine's phone beeped.

'The girls want to meet me at the tavern, so count me out,' she said, pocketing her mobile and scraping back the chair.

'Why can't we just get takeaway?' Stephen said.

'Don't you want to hear the news?' Susie said. They both stared at her. She felt like a speaker in parliament delivering boring dialogue.

'I had a call from your father's solicitor and he's sending a letter to you about your entitlements. It seems Doug had very little in the bank but he owns a house. Do you remember that house we lived in for a while at Hurtsville Grove? You kids were still pretty little. Apparently it is free of a mortgage so if Petria agrees, it can be sold, and you'll get a third share each. It's probably worth a bit now.'

'Mum. I don't want his filthy drug money. You can have it. I couldn't justify using it,' Jasmine said.

'That house was bought long before he got involved in drugs so you don't have to worry.'

'I'll be rich,' Stephen said. 'I'll be able to quit school and bum around for a while. How cool.'

'Oh no you won't,' Susie half-laughed. 'It's most likely your share will go into a trust fund till you're 18. That's what usually happens.'

'What? No way. That can't be right. That's not fair,' Stephen grumbled.

'Poor Stevo,' Jasmine laughed. 'You had it all spent before you even got it.'

'Shut up. Anyway, if you were any sort of sister you'd lend me some of yours.' He started walking off down the hall.

'As if. In your dreams buddy,' Jasmine called after him.

The girls had arranged to meet Jasmine at Caloundra because she always seemed to be the one driving up the coast to see them. The tavern was set back from the beach but the building was high enough so that you could get glimpses of the surf rolling in. The sun had almost gone but the sky looked grey, with pinkish low lying clouds draped like a blanket over Moreton Island. They found a table on the open veranda. It was still warm weather, but the evenings brought a refreshing coolness. Amanda looked happy and relaxed after her honeymoon and Megan was her usual effervescent self.

It's just what I need. Laughs and happy times with my friends. God knows I haven't had much of that lately.

They listened as Amanda told them about Vanuatu. 'It's a third world country. But the people are so nice. And the food...' She blew her cheeks out. 'I'll have to go to Boot Camp again.' They all laughed. Megan talked about work and how they were training the new girl at the photo shop.

'She's a pretty little thing but no brains really. The other girls complain that she forgets how to do things and she stuffs up orders. She's always running off to the bathroom to redo her hair or make-up. We need you back Jaz.' Both girls turned their eyes to Jasmine.

'Come on Jaz. Now it's your turn spit it out. We need all the details,' Amanda said. Jasmine had already told the girls about the dramas, but she hadn't elaborated much. She swallowed. It was hard to go over it all again. She just wanted it to all go away. She managed to choke out a few of the events of the past week. But she felt like a fool. She'd got sucked in totally.

'So that Brad guy was right. Andy is a druggo.'

'Yep,' Jasmine said, tears just waiting to burst out. 'How could I have been so stupid? I trusted him. And now....and now I'm the one made out to be the guilty one.'

'I always thought that Andy was too good to be true,' Megan said. 'Now we know.'

'Oh Jaz,' Amanda said. 'I thought he was going to be the man of your dreams. What an arsehole. How could he betray you like that?'

They sipped their drinks in silence for a while. Amanda stood and adjusted her skirt. 'Shit look at my belly. Either this skirt has shrunk or I'm preggers.' They all giggled. She wriggled back into the chair. 'Anyway let's change the subject. Tell us about this new sister of yours.'

SEVENTEEN

Christine agreed with Jasmine that pelican paintings and photos would be a hit. 'I've got lots of small paintings that I've done of pelicans. It would be great if I could sell them at the markets and part of the proceeds could go to the Rescue Centre,' Jasmine said.

'It would be a great away to raise public awareness. Not many people know about us and the work we do,' Christine said.

'You know what would be good,' Jasmine continued. 'I've seen this on web pages. People can "Adopt a Pelican". They would pay a nominated amount, receive a photo and a monthly newsletter. It would help pay for the food or other things the birds need in their recovery. What do you think?'

'Brilliant Jasmine. But we would need someone to coordinate all that. I couldn't do it on my own.'

'It's okay. I can cover the market side of it. We just need someone to help with the webpage and someone to organise the newsletter.'

'Yeah. It's not that easy. But starting out with the pictures would be great. Thanks so much.'

Jasmine hadn't felt this motivated for months. Now she had a cause worth working for. The Sunday market was always a popular place. It was held in the main street and there were stall holders selling a variety of products; clothing, pottery, crafts, pet fish, second hand books, bric-a brac, sarongs, plants, jewellery and food. It would take her mind off the dramas of the past weeks. On her stall she would set up her small paintings on easels and use the enlargements of the photos she'd taken of the " patients" at the Rescue Service.

Christine had some brochures that could be given out. She said she could come and help on the first day if she could get Phil to cover for her at the Centre. When she arrived home and Susie heard the plans, she offered to help when she could.

Things were all falling into place... and then Jasmine read her Facebook page.

She couldn't believe it. Her face drained of colour and a buzzing sound filled her head. Andy had posted several nasty comments slamming Jasmine as a 'slut' and someone who couldn't be trusted, someone who dealt in drugs. All her friends would read this. *God the creep.* She threw herself onto her pillow and cried.

Susie heard the sobs and came in. She couldn't believe it either.

'Don't worry, Jaz. He's just being nasty because he's in a mess himself. As if your friends would believe that. They know you. He's only dug the hole deeper for himself.'

If Jasmine had even a smidgen of hope that she would reunite with Andy, that was blown up now. *He can rot in hell. I hope the cops grab him and he gets what he deserves.*

Jasmine returned to work at the zoo on Thursday but she went about her work in a mechanical fashion. She felt on edge in case she would see Andy. Just about everything the new girl did annoyed her and she had to bite her tongue and walk away. At lunchtime she met up with Megan and they walked over to the cafe to see Amanda.

'Do you know Andy's left?' Amanda said as she wiped down one of the tables. It was the lunchtime crowd and busy so she wouldn't be joining them for lunch.

'When? What happened?' Megan said.

'Brian just came by here and told me. He finished up yesterday. Boss didn't like his attitude. Good riddance I say.'

'Thank God. I don't think I could keep working with that prick around,' Jasmine said.

'I can't believe he'd be so low to write that stuff about you,' Amanda said. 'Anyway I must get back behind the counter. What do you girls want?' They ordered salad wraps and drinks and sat themselves down in a corner away from the noisy family groups. It was another clear, fine day which always brought out the crowds. Just opposite to where they sat was the camel enclosure. The girls watched as a family group walked leisurely past then paused as an old hairy camel stuck his head over the high fence. He stretched his bristly neck out and with his rubber lips grabbed the little boy's cap. 'Hey,' the little kid yelled. 'Give it back.' Everyone was laughing as the camel slobbered over the hat and then, realising it was not edible, dropped it to the ground. That was the good thing about working at the zoo. There were always things to observe or laugh at. Just being around animals was stimulating and calming at the same time.

Jasmine finished work early. It had been a quiet day and, because she was still considered casual, her supervisor told her to go home. She was relieved. The traumatic events lately had drained her and she felt exhausted.

As she walked up the stairs of the cottage she felt a veil of fear slip down and she shivered. Something was not right. But what? She opened the door with her key and slowly pushed it. Nothing. She stepped into the house as if on egg shells. Her eyes drank in the room, nothing amiss. The only sound was the monotonous tick of the kitchen clock.

She let out a sigh. *Why am I so edgy? I'm my own worst enemy. That's what mum reckons too.* Heading to her room she kicked off her shoes. Then she froze. The bedroom looked like a tornado had hit it. The bedclothes were ripped and tossed, every drawer was open or pulled right out with clothes hanging in agony. Her paintings and art materials were strewn in an arc of destruction. Posters were ripped down and her figurine collection lay scattered on the floor, some pieces broken beyond repair. She held her hand to her mouth, barely breathing, her body not able to deal with this awful tableau.

Her eyes stung and she felt numb. *What else has been violated?* She slowly turned and then she was hit with it. Written in streaked lipstick, messy letters on the wall spelt it out.

YOU'LL PAY BITCH.

She sank to her knees and heard an animal sound. It was coming from her own throat. Then she scrambled up panicking. *What if he's still here? Shit.* She raced for the front door grabbing her bag on the way. Once she reached the car she tried to steady herself, then she called Susie, voice and body still trembling.

Susie was furious. It was obvious to both of them that this was Andy's work as Jasmine's room was the only one trashed.

Susie called the police and while they waited, they sipped coffee and tried to calm each other.

'This is becoming quite a habit,' Sergeant Gray said with a smile, when he arrived accompanied by two officers who were armed with cameras and a fingerprint kit. Susie and Jasmine remained silent.

'So have you touched or moved anything?' Gray asked. Jasmine shook her head. The police checked the back door and windows, and then the print technicians went to work.

'Whoever did this certainly had a bee in his bonnet about something,' Sergeant Gray said. 'Who do you think that might be?'

'Andy,' Jasmine said softly. 'Andy Pascoe.'

'And why do you think he'd do that?'

Jasmine shrugged. 'He's the only one I know who'd hate me that much.'

'Why would that be?'

Jasmine told him about the drug episodes, the stalking, the messages and her rejection of him.

'Well,' Gray said flipping over a page in his notebook, 'Sounds like it might be him. Has this ever happened before?'

Both women shook their heads. 'We'll see if we can match the prints. I believe we now have his prints on our system.'

The print technicians came out holding bags and nodded at Sergeant Gray. He picked up his hat and hitched his trousers.

'If the prints are Andy's he'll be charged with wilful damage. We can't find evidence of a break-in. Windows and doors don't appear to be tampered with. For all we know he might have been a regular visitor. Had the door open for him. Know what I mean?' He raised his bushy eyebrows.

Jasmine frowned and sat up. 'What? What do you mean?'

'What are you getting at Sergeant?' Susie stormed, her hands on her hips. 'He wasn't welcome here. He's broken in and done all this. He was stalking Jasmine. Harassing her. Didn't she just tell you that?'

'Did he ever threaten you?' Gray asked, directing his attention to Jasmine.

'Don't you call that bloody lipstick message a threat? For God's sake,' Susie shouted. The officers started to back out.

'We'll let you know about the prints. If it is Andy we advise you to take out an AVO.' He tipped his hat and left.

Stephen sprinted in as the police drove off. He stared at Susie and Jasmine. 'What just happened?'

'Don't ask,' Susie said putting her head in her hands. Jasmine just sat and stared.

EIGHTEEN

Brad stood on the bow letting his body move in sync with the constant motion of the trawling vessel as they made their way home. Seabirds screeched and wheeled around the boat. In the distance he could just make out white clusters on the shore, glimpses of humanity. This week on the boat seemed to go on forever. He thought of Jasmine, dreamed of Jasmine. He didn't know why, he didn't know her all that well. She just seemed so vulnerable and he didn't want her being hurt, caught up in Andy's lies. Jasmine didn't tell him the whole story, but he figured out most of it from what the cops had implied. He wondered if they'd got Johnno yet. He seemed to be the master mind behind it all.

His thoughts went to his mum and he wondered how she was coping. Nick, the other deck hand, had a father who was a Vietnam vet too. He'd lent Brad a book called "Ashes of Vietnam" and said that it might help him understand what went on all those years ago. But Brad was not much of a reader and the book was still in his cupboard waiting for someone to open it. Thoughts of his father only stirred up the fire in his gut. Lots of men went to Vietnam and other wars. They didn't all end up like this surely. He could see no excuse for the emotional abuse, the selfishness, the ravings of a madman. But it hadn't always been that bad. He remembered good times when he was young when the family was reasonably stable, and his father worked, kept busy and mixed with others. He did what most fathers did, took them camping, fishing, to the beach. There were games of footy and cricket. But it started to go sour as he grew. He could never live up to his father's expectations, whatever they were. His mother tried to compensate but that was merely a bandaid solution. The put-downs and rejection scarred him for life, he'd been too young to rationalise what was happening. Jacko's sharp voice snapped him out of his thoughts. "Get ya finger out boys." He took a deep breath and went down below to start preparing the crates.

He called Jasmine when he arrived back at Mooloolaba and they arranged to meet at the boat ramp near her home the next morning.

'You won't tell me off again like the first time will you?' Brad asked over the phone.

'Not if you behave,' she joked.

As Brad pulled up at the boat ramp car park, he saw Jasmine on the sandy shore surrounded by pelicans. Her hair was loose and she was wearing shorts and a short t-shirt. Sometimes she looked like a little girl, a delicate mermaid. She glanced over and waved.

She helped Brad as he manoeuvred the trailer down the ramp, then standing in thigh deep water, she held the tinnie steady while he drove the trailer back to park it.

'How come you're so expert at this?' Brad asked.

'You forget I went fishing with my grandfather heaps of times when I was on holidays.'

'Yeah. That's right. I should just lie back and you can take over.'

Jasmine smiled as he helped her aboard. His hand felt rough but strong. The energy seemed to pulse through her veins. Why did she feel like this? She felt safe, safer than she had for some time.

Soon they were zipping across the water, the wind raking their hair. Jasmine sat up front, held her hat and gazed ahead. Brad's eyes followed the lines of her body, down the slender arms, past her petite hips, and down to those long, smooth legs. His body tingled as he imagined running his hands over her body. She turned to smile at him, the wind whipping her hair and plastering it to her face. Brad eased the engine. They had travelled south and were now approaching the mouth of Bell's Creek. The narrow, deep green creek was lined with mangroves and it felt like they were entering a fantasy world as they motored in and soaked up the silence. A gangly legged egret alighted on a tea tree branch and watched them from his perch. All it needed now were swirls of mist.

'I remember this place. Grandpa used to drop crab pots here.'

'We'll pull up and drop a line in. See what happens.' Brad stopped the motor and dropped anchor. He got the lines ready and started threading a worm on Jasmine's hook.

'No. I can do it,' she said reaching for the line. Her hand brushed Brad's, and they locked eyes but only for a second.

'Well you can do mine too. I'll just relax.' Brad made himself comfortable in his seat, stretched his legs and put his hands behind his head. There was that dimpled smile again.

'Yeah right Buddy. Do your own,' Jasmine laughed. She felt relaxed out here. It was the best thing, away from everyone and everything that had caused her angst in the past weeks. And she didn't feel pressured to talk about it.

Apart from the occasional passing boat they were on their own. Waiting. Jasmine knew fishing required a great deal of patience.

'How was your week on the trawler?' she asked, her eyes following the fishing line into the emerald water.

'Yeah okay I guess. I'm always glad to get home though. I'm thinking of getting another job. I'm sick of working away.'

'What would you do?'

'I could try the Fisheries...or the mines. They make shitloads there.'

'But you'd still be away.'

'Yeah but I'd live there. Make a go of it. I think I'm ready for a change of scenery. What about you? Are you happy with your job?'

Jasmine brushed some wisps of hair behind her ear. 'In some ways I am. I really want to work in the animal hospital there. But I'd have to study to get a position.'

'Why don't you?'Brad asked scratching and hitting at his neck. 'Bloody mossies.' Luckily Jasmine had plastered insect repellent on, so she hadn't been bitten yet.

'Well it looks like I might be able to now. I've contacted the uni and I can start a part time course in June.'

'Cool.' Brad paused. 'Hey tell me, any more dramas this week?'

Jasmine looked away and sighed. 'You could say that,' she said softly.

Brad bent forward and brushed her leg. 'Hey you don't have to talk about it. It's okay.'

Jasmine turned to face him and fell into those deep eyes of his. She went through recent events; the drug charge, the stalking, the break-in. Brad could see it pained her to talk about it.

'Holy crap. That bastard. The cops should have him locked up by now. You must be shit scared with that nutter on the loose.'

'I've decided to move in with Megan, another girl from work. Her flatmate Sara has moved to Melbourne. I'm hoping he won't find me there. It gives me the creeps thinking he's out there. Who knows what he's planning next.'

'You shouldn't have to move because of that arsehole.'

'I was moving out anyway. Need to have my own place. Mum is too much of a drama queen.'

'So you live with your mum?'

'And my teenage brother Stephen. That's a real hoot.' She rolled her eyes. 'What about your parents? Where are they?'

'The olds are in Mooloolaba. Not far from my flat. I don't have any brothers or sisters though.'

Jasmine's line jerked and she jumped. 'I think I have something,' she said reeling in a good sized whiting which was flapping flashes of silver in the sunlight. As it dropped in the boat, she leapt around shrieking and laughing nearly capsizing the boat. Brad reefed the hook out and threw the slippery fish into the bucket.

'Sit down woman,' he joked and Jasmine lost her footing and fell on her bum laughing. Then his line went off. Jasmine watched as he hauled the line in, his muscly upper arm and wave tattoo just visible under his flannel sleeve.He added another fish to their bucket. He washed his hands in the salt water, heaved the anchor up, and started the motor.

'I'm starving. Let's pull up somewhere and have something.'

'Did you bring some food?'

'Look in the esky,' Brad said nodding to the blue chest beside him. Jasmine lifted the lid. Under some towels were takeaway salad rolls and some cola drinks. *What a man. He's thought of everything.*

'How about we pull up at Bribie,' Brad yelled above the noise of the motor. Jasmine nodded and smiled.

The Passage was busy now that it was nearly midday. There were small motor boats whizzing past and sailboats with their colourful sails making good use of the breeze. Over near the boardwalk she could see kite surfers leaping and skimming over the waves.

This felt just like the old days when she picnicked here with her grandfather on Bribie's northern shores. They pulled the boat into a little cove and tied it to a broken tree limb jutting out into the water. Brad spread the towels on a grassy sand ledge and they enjoyed their meal all the while savouring the view. A kookaburra sat in a nearby acacia tilting his head as he searched for a meal. Pelicans and seagulls huddled on a sandbank in the middle of the passage.

'We could probably walk right out there to those birds,' Brad said.

'Come on then. Let's go,' Jasmine said packing up the wrappings and empty drink bottles.

They started wading out. The water remained at about thigh level for a distance of 50 metres or so, and then all that separated them from the birds was a deeper channel about 20 metres wide.

'Damn,' Jasmine said scanning for a shallower section. 'Ah well it looks like we'll get wet.' She ploughed in, grabbing Brad's strong muscular arm, and they fell into the cool turquoise channel together, kicking and yelling. Birds took off in a spray of brilliant white.

'Now look what you've done,' Brad said as they swam towards the sandy island. They flopped onto the sandbank, puffing and laughing.

'They'll come back. Look at those guys over there,' Jasmine said gazing at the pelicans snoozing or grooming themselves. Sea gulls strutted around looking for a meal, or yo-yoed and screeched in the air above. 'God look at us. We're like a pair of drowned rats. It's bloody cold too.' She rubbed her arms up and down.

Brad looked at Jasmine sitting cross-legged on the sand. Her wet t-shirt now stuck to her neat breasts, beads of water glistened on her skin and her wet hair clung to her head, a few wayward locks framing her face. He could grab her right now. She was so desirable, so sexy. He took a deep breath and stared back at the beach.

'Jaz, are you going back to Andy?'

'What?' She frowned and stared at him.

'Will you go back with Andy?' Brad was playing with the sand, picking up handfuls and dropping them in heaps.

'Why would you ask me that?'

'Well. I don't know. I guess he's done all that crap. But maybe you still have feelings for him.'

'I don't want to see that creep again.' Jasmine looked out over the water. 'Why would you even think that...that I'd want to be with him?'

'He's got charm. Maybe part of you believes he's innocent, couldn't help it, or he might change.'

'No. No. I don't think that.' Her brow furrowed even deeper.

'Well you didn't believe me. I tried to warn you.'

Jasmine stood up straight. 'So is that it?' She fumed, glaring at him. 'You think I'm a weak shit. I'll be sucked in again.'

'No...I---'

'It's time we left,' she snapped. She slipped into the water and swam off. Brad looked at the birds and shrugged.

An angry and confused silence descended on the boat as they headed back to the boat ramp. Jasmine sat huddled on the middle seat, a towel wrapped tightly around her. Brad stared ahead.

They unpacked the gear and winched the boat back on the trailer.

'I'm going to fillet these fish before I go home,' Brad said walking over to the filleting table. 'You're going to stay aren't you? Then you can take the fillets home.' Jasmine shrugged and sat on the rock wall watching the pelicans start arriving, drawn like magnets to the little cove with the hope of a free feed. They flapped and snapped, pushing at each other and grunting when Brad threw the scraps.

When he was done he wrapped the fillets up and washed his hands. Jasmine thanked him when he gave her the fish, but straightaway she started walking to her car.

'Jaz. Wait.'

She stopped but didn't face him.

'I'm a dickhead. Sorry.'

She turned. 'Thanks for the trip...and the lunch,' she said softly. Brad followed her to the car.

'I'll call later,' he said as she closed the door and drove off. He ran his hand through his stiff, salty curls. *Oh man. What a fuckhead. Now she's pissed off with me. What did I do? What did I say?* Then he had another thought. *Maybe she was more involved than she made out. The cops certainly thought so. Maybe she was in deep shit and trying to cover up. Who bloody knows? She wouldn't listen to me anyhow.*

NINETEEN

It was Sunday and Sergeant Gray did not feel like being here at the meeting. His wife and kids were used to his unusual shifts but he was getting tired of it, especially weekend work. But this was an important case. They were getting close to cracking another drug ring.

He shook hands with the two detectives Baker and Summers. They were joined by a new red-haired female detective who they introduced as Amelia Price. She appeared to have a manner that matched her hair. Not one to get on the wrong side of, Gray thought.

Two young plain-clothed men came through the door carrying files. They were the surveillance officers, Chris and Sam.

'Come on through,' Gray said ushering them down the hall.

'Janice,' he addressed the young constable on the front desk. 'Can you bring some coffees in? Ta.'

After they had all settled in the meeting room, Summers shuffled some papers, rubbed his moustache and looked at Gray. 'You probably know we got John Baxter, aka Johnno.' The sergeant nodded. 'As arranged, Sam and Chris here have been covering Andrew Pascoe.' He nodded towards the two men. 'I'll hand over to them and they can outline his movements.'

There was a soft tap at the door and Janice came in with a tray of steaming coffees, milk in a jug and sachets of sugar. They handed the mugs around.

The officer called Chris opened his book and began to read out his findings.

'We've been staking out the resort where Pascoe lives. We started yesterday morning at 9am. I watch the front entrance/ exit while Sam does the carpark and back entrance/ exit. It seems your boy Andy is lying low. He leaves the unit to go surfing, and he goes to the bottle shop and pub. He rarely goes home alone though. Always a young girl in tow. He's one busy boy, drinking and screwing. There were muffled laughs. Amelia scowled.

'What about the girl Jasmine? Has he gone back to her place since the break-in on Friday? Has she seen him?' Gray asked.

'Not since we've been on to him,' Chris said.

'I don't know why she hasn't taken an AVO out on him. From what she told us he's one mad cookie and unpredictable. She still insists she was set up,' Sergeant Gray said.

'We have noticed something disturbing,' Sam said. 'There are others watching Andy Pascoe's movements. A man and a woman. We see them at the pub sitting in the same corner. They also sit in a car outside the resort. The woman often walks in, sits in the foyer, then uses her phone. She's bottle blonde, slim build, about 40.He's a bit older, stocky, bit of a beer gut, very distinctive long greyish beard, tattoos on both arms. She wears hippy type clothing, he wears bikie gear.'

'What about the vehicle?' Detective Brady asked.

'That's the thing. They use a black four wheel drive and a Harley bike,' Chris said.

'Have you checked the regos yet?' Brady asked.

'Not yet. We only just realised they were always around and were using the 4WD as well as the bike,' Sam said.

'Well, let's get onto that straight away,' Brady said taking a sip of coffee.

'My guess is that this Andy's still got money or drugs or both, and these guys are after it,' Summers said sitting back in his chair.

'Should we do another search?' Brady asked.

'No. We've done that and he's onto us. He's planted stuff somewhere else I'm sure of it,' Summers said. 'We talked to the last flat mate Bradley Nash. Might be wise to search that place too.'

'What about the girl Jasmine?' red-haired Amelia said. They all looked at her. 'You said she had drugs in her bag. You found a bag of cash in her car. Why aren't you onto her? She's probably hiding stuff for him.'

Gray shook his head. 'I doubt it. I think she's been an innocent pawn in all of this. He stalked her, trashed her house. He wouldn't be the flavour of the month.' He chewed his pen. 'But you're right, we can't discount it.'

They all agreed to continue the surveillance, check the regos on the suspicious vehicle and bike, and arrange more searches.

Jasmine packed the last of her boxes into her little green Honda. She was excited about moving in with Megan. The unit was at Buddina on a neck of land with the beach on one side and the canal on the other. It was much quieter there than Mooloolaba, and the good thing was that there was a park on the canals with walkways and outdoor gym equipment. The main walkway skirted the canal and snaked its way up to the Point Cartwright lighthouse.

The canal was a busy waterway with boats coming from and going to the ocean. The bigger yachts and trawlers docked at the Mooloolaba Marina not far in from the harbour entrance. She'd seen pelicans there too. It wouldn't be as quiet as Golden Beach but she could still go back to her special place when she visited her mum.

Susie came out to say good bye. The tears pushed at her lids but she held back. She didn't want to upset Jasmine. They hugged for a long time.

'Mum. I'm only going up to Buddina. I'm only 15 minutes away.'

'Now have you got those frozen meals I made for you? And what about the bed linen? Did you get that?'

'Yes Mum. Say bye to Stephen for me.'

'He should be here to see you off. I told him when you were going.'

'Don't worry Mum. He's probably out partying. He doesn't have to share stuff anymore. He can have the bathroom all to himself.' She started the engine and drove off, tooting the horn and waving out of the window. When she turned the corner she saw her mum out on the kerb still waving.

Susie couldn't help it. She burst into tears. *I hope she'll be okay. It's tough out there. But she's old enough and it will be good for her. I'll really miss her though.*

She grabbed some tissues and put the kettle on. She sat at the kitchen table and turned on her laptop. She brought up the internet and typed in "Dating Services". *What am I doing? This is crazy.* One of her single friends Helen had suggested this. She'd just met a really nice guy on an internet dating site and they were seeing each other regularly. Helen was about her age and was feeling lonely. She said she wanted someone to go out walking with, someone to dance with, someone to accompany her on trips. 'If the friendship develops into something deeper well that's fine,' she said. 'If it doesn't what have I lost? I'm taking it a day at a time.'

Susie liked that idea. She did get lonely. And now Jasmine had gone the chasm was deeper. *Soon Stephen will head off too. Then where will I be? Just me looking at four walls.*

The kettle boiled and she made the coffee, white with only a half a spoon of sugar. She was cutting back on the sweets. It had always been a problem for her especially now she was watching her weight. She had her father to blame. He was a real sweet tooth.

As she walked past the front window she saw a silver car pull up. It'd be Mark's dad Cameron dropping Stephen back. They'd all been to the soccer match at Kawana where the boys played in the "Rebels" team. Stephen was thinking of giving it up because he wanted to spend more time surfing, but Susie hoped he wouldn't. It was a more social activity than surfing and she believed teenagers needed that. She glanced at the clock.2.30.Her friend Jan would be here soon to take her to the squash courts. The gym work was keeping her fit but she still wanted to lose more kilos. It seemed to be getting harder and harder these days to shift the extra weight. She'd never had to watch her weight before she'd had the kids, but then the pregnancies, the hormones and some bad eating habits had added a bit of fat. Well she'd blame that anyway.

She heard the footsteps on the stairs and voices. Then she remembered the laptop. She quickly logged off the dating site. Stephen and Mark stomped in with their duffle bags over their shoulders, followed closely by Cameron.

'Mum. Mark's staying. Can you drop him home later?' Stephen asked.

'Sure, but I'll be at squash till about five. Is that okay?'

A distant voice called, 'Yep.'

She turned to Cameron. 'Hi Cam. How are you?'

'Good. Good.'

'Would you like a quick coffee? I have to leave around three.'

'Yeah. That'd be great thanks.' He pulled out a chair and folded his lanky frame into it. She had known Cameron for a number of years, ever since the boys became friends at high school. He was doing it tough trying to bring up two boys on his own. His wife, Genevieve, had met another man at her workplace and they'd gone off together. The last she heard they were in America somewhere. It seemed that the marriage had been rocky for a while, so Cameron had been going through a long grieving process. In some ways that was what it was like, the loss of a partner to someone else, like a death, only add to it rejection and deception. And she could relate to that. She had many conversations with Cameron about how they were both feeling and she had become very close to him. But she knew it was no use getting too involved when he was still in love with Genevieve. He was an imposing character, tall, slim, dark hair that flicked up at the front. When he smiled he had elongated dimples on either side of his mouth. Captivating.

'So how did the game go?'

'A draw. They played well. Both sides did.' He paused. 'Stephen told me that Jasmine has left home.'

'Yes,' Susie said bringing his coffee over. 'She's been wanting to move out for a while. I'll miss her though.'

'Well she's not that far away. At least she's not overseas.'

'No I'm glad of that.'

'Has all that police stuff settled down?' Cameron asked taking a sip of coffee.

'God. I hope so. You heard about the break-in?'

'Stevo said something about it.'

'This Andy guy trashed Jasmine's room. He wouldn't leave her alone, kept stalking her.'

'What are the police doing about it?'

'Not much. They matched his prints and charged him with wilful damage. But he's still out there. Who knows what he's capable of.'

'You have to be so careful these days. You try to warn your kids but they don't always listen.'

They heard a car pull up and Susie went to the window.

'Jan's here. Sorry Cam.' He finished the last few mouthfuls and Susie rinsed the mugs. He stood up and started for the door.

'Why don't you come too?' Susie asked.

'What? Ah no.' He glanced down at his sneakers.

'They'll do. You play squash don't you?'

Cameron smiled his winning smile. 'I'd love to,' he said.

TWENTY

Andy put his feet up on the railing of his new unit and took a swig of beer. He'd have to get out of here soon. Things were hotting up. The cops were onto him and now that bitch Jasmine had turned on him too. He'd heard that Johnno had been charged and was out on bail. He should never have listened to that prick. Totally used, that's how he felt. He didn't know how many others were in on it, but he was sure the mob would be after him. They probably thought he'd dobbed them in or given the cops information. But it was Jasmine's rejection that hurt the most. He gritted his teeth. *I haven't finished with you yet you bitch.*

'Andy,' a small voice called. He turned. The blonde chick was standing there in her underwear an innocent look on her face. 'Come back to bed Babe.' He reached for her and she sat on his lap. Their mouths met and he nearly swallowed her. He grabbed her breast and felt himself go hard. Picking her up in his arms, he raced her off to the bedroom. She was some hot sex kitten.

Andy was fast running out of cash. He needed to get to his secret cache. But he had to get the timing right. He'd been deliberately lying low in case some of Johnno's mates were tracking him. He had spent the weekend surfing, relaxing and drinking. No chance of being followed to the old flat if the car stayed in the car park. There didn't seem to be anyone suspicious stalking him.

The young girl Katie was in the shower, so when she left, he'd implement his next move. It would be best he thought if he packed up, loaded his gear in the car and headed off down south till things cooled off. He had the lease on the unit for six months so he could always come back. But first he had things to deal with, the money and that bitch Jasmine.

Jasmine couldn't understand why Brad was so judgemental, so patronising. She really liked the guy but he had a way of putting fuel on the flames. *How could he even think I'd go back to Andy? As if I'm some sort of weak little bimbo. He probably thinks I'm into the drug thing with Andy... But maybe he was sussing things out. Maybe he just wants to protect me.* She decided to call on him. Clear the air. She didn't want to lose his friendship.

When she called at Brad's place there was no answer to her knock so she walked down the side of the building. He was out the back bringing in some sad looking washing. There were no pegs. How could guys just throw the clothes over the line like that? He nearly dropped the clothes basket.

'Jaz. God. I didn't expect you.'

'Hi, I came for a quick chat.'

'Come on in,' he said opening the back screen door. 'How's things?'

'Yeah good. I've moved out of home.'

'Already? Where's your new place?'

'Buddina. It's nice and modern, right near La Balsa Park.'

'Right.' He plonked the basket in the lounge and went to the fridge. 'Like a drink?'

'A cola if you have one.' Brad grabbed a cola and a beer and they went into the lounge. Jasmine sat on the sofa, and he settled on the single wonky chair. Uncertainty hung in the air.

'I...About yesterday...' Jasmine stumbled.

'Jaz, You--'

'No. Let me finish.' Jasmine twisted her hands. 'I had a great time...really. But I'm sorry I snapped.'

'It's okay Jaz.' Brad got up and sat with her his huge arm around her shoulders. 'You were right I should mind my own business.' She looked up at him and fell into those warm eyes. Her whole body sensed his closeness, his smell, his breath. When their lips met it was soft and sensuous. Her heart pumped faster and she felt the warmth envelop her like a candle burning from within. She rested her head on his chest and nuzzled into his neck. The arms that held her tightened and she felt safe again.

'I hope you don't have to go out on the boat for a while.'

'Tomorrow morning.'

Jasmine sat up with a pout. 'Oh no. We were just starting.'

He kissed her again, this time it was long and lingering. He kissed her hair, her eyes, her ears until she squirmed and giggled.

Andy couldn't believe it when he pulled up at the flat. *What the fuck? Jasmine's car. What's she doing here? And that prick Brad what's he up to?* No chance to get inside and get the cash now but he could deal with her one last time, the moll.

He jumped from the car but stopped as a black 4WD screeched to a halt beside him. He noticed a blonde woman in the passenger seat. He seized up with fear. A bearded bikie-looking man jumped out of the driver's side, came towards him and grabbed his shirt.

'Where's the cash Fuckhead?' he said in a gravelly voice.

'I don't have it. It's---' The bikie's massive fist scrunched the shirt tighter and Andy was nearly lifted off his feet. Then he felt the cold metal pressing against his chest. His eyes widened and his throat constricted.

'Let. Me. Go. I'll get it,' he choked. The bikie turned him around and followed him towards the stairs, the pistol pressed firmly against his back.

'Hurry up Arsewipe.'

Jasmine and Brad came to the door with puzzled looks on their faces. Andy grabbed Jasmine and swung her around in front of him.

'You want me. Then you can take her first,' he screamed.

Two rapid shots rang out and Jasmine and Andy crumpled to the floor. The bearded man raced off, and he and his blonde took off in a shower of gravel, another car in hot pursuit.

Brad let out a silent scream. It was as if everything was happening in slow motion and he was numbed.

'Jaz. Shit. Jaz.' He rolled Andy's lifeless body off her. Blood was plastered to her shirt from Andy's chest wound. Her eyes were flickering and she moaned.

'My leg. Brad, my leg.' She was clutching her right thigh where blood was seeping between her fingers, and pooling around the hole in her shorts. He ripped his t-shirt off and wrapped it tightly around the wound.

'It's okay,' he said puffing. 'I'll call for help.' He brushed her hair back from her face and kissed her cheek. 'Hang in there Babe.'

Then he heard the sirens and looked up. An ambulance and a police patrol car had rounded the corner, pulled up lights flashing and sirens screaming. A few people had started to gather in the street, some with their hands to their mouths. Someone was quick calling the ambos. He was so grateful. This was a nightmare, like a scene from CSI on TV. He knelt beside Jasmine as the paramedics did their job. He felt helpless, naked. He held his arms around his chest and shivered. Jasmine had her eyes closed. They'd given her an injection and now she was on a drip.

More police vehicles arrived as the dusk descended and the flashing lights seemed to turn the street into a Christmas light show. The paramedics and police used Jasmine's phone and they were able to contact Susie. Brad was asked what seemed like a trillion questions.

The ambulance left with Jasmine on board but Brad barely had time to watch. He was ushered inside while they moved Andy's body and three detectives came in to question him further. He went to the bathroom to wash his bloodied hands, and they watched as he rummaged in the washing basket for a t-shirt, and slipped it on. They introduced themselves. Brady and Summers he knew, but the red-haired woman was new. They sat themselves in the lounge. Brad offered them drinks but they declined.

The moustached one called Summers spoke first. 'Can you run through the events as you witnessed them?'

'Will it take long? I want to get to the hospital to see how Jasmine is.'

'We'll make it as quick as we can. Now start.'

Brad took a breath. 'Jasmine came over---'

'And Jasmine is?'

'A friend. She's a friend.'

Summers nodded while Brady took notes.

'She wasn't here long when we heard two cars pull up and angry voices outside. We both went to the front door. Andy was coming towards the stairs with a panicked look on his face and a bearded guy was following right up close as if he was holding Andy's shirt or something.'

'Can you describe this bearded guy?'

'He looked like a bikie type. Big build, tattoos on his arms. His beard was long, grey. He wore a beanie type hat. I can't remember much because I was looking at Andy wondering what the hell he was doing here.'

'Did you hear any conversation?'

'Andy yelled, "I'll get it", then there was nothing until he grabbed Jasmine.'

'Continue,' Summers said.

'Andy lunged at Jasmine and spun her around. It all happened so fast.' He paused and shook his head. 'Andy yelled something like, "Take her first". Then I heard what seemed like two shots. I was in shock. Jasmine and Andy fell down and the bearded guy took off. And I mean took off. He was like lightning, man. I saw what looked like a gun in his hand but my main concern was Jasmine.'

'What do you remember of the vehicle?'

'It was a black 4WD. And...and there was a blonde woman in the passenger seat.'

'What about the gun?'

'I didn't see much, a flash of metal. It was smallish like a pistol.'

'Then what happened?'Summers said.

The red-haired detective shifted in her chair and brushed her hair back.

'I rolled Andy off Jasmine. I could see his chest wound so I had a fair idea he was dead. The blood had soaked onto Jasmine's shirt. I checked her and found a bullet wound on her thigh. I wrapped my t-shirt around it, like a tourniquet.'

'Was she conscious?'

'Yes. She said her leg hurt.'

'How did you know Andy?'

'He used to flat here. He left recently.'

'Why do you think he was coming to the flat?'

Brad shrugged. 'I don't know. He'd collected all his things. There was no reason I know of.'

'Do you think he was after Jasmine?'

'Could have been. But hc didn't know she'd be here.'

'Are you aware that Andy had been stalking Jasmine?'

'Yes. She told me.'

Brady took over. 'Had you ever seen this bearded guy before?'

'No.'

'When Andy said "I'll get it", what did you think he meant?'

'I don't know.'

'Were you aware of any drug activity when Andy lived here?'

'You guys have already questioned me about that. He smoked pot and I did think his behaviour was strange sometimes. He was always receiving calls and driving off at all hours. But I kept to myself. I work out on the trawler most of the week so I didn't see a lot.'

'Do you think Andy stashed drugs or money on these premises?'

'Not that I know of.'

'Could he have come here while you were away? Did he have a key?

'I wouldn't know if he came here. I didn't see any evidence of it. But yes he probably still had a key.'

Brady stood and the others followed. As he pocketed his notebook he said, 'We will have to search the premises and you will have to find somewhere else to spend the night. The place is now a crime scene.'

Later as he drove off to the hospital he hoped and prayed that Jasmine would be okay. *That idiot Andy. Everywhere he went lately he caused trouble. The dickhead. And look where it got him. A cold slab in the mortuary.* He felt sick as he replayed the shooting scenario in his head. *Who was that bearded guy? What had Andy done that was so bad? What were they after? I didn't like Andy's behaviour lately, but no one deserved to be gunned down like that. It could have been Jasmine...or me. What a fuckin' mess.*

TWENTY- ONE

Susie got the call just as she returned from squash games with her friends. She and Cameron arrived home sweating and laughing, and then everything seemed to crash around them. The police had given her some details of the shooting, but she wasn't really taking it in. Stephen and Mark said they'd be fine so Cameron offered to drive her to the hospital. She was drained of colour and shaking.

'I can't believe it,' she kept saying. 'How could something like this happen? The fucking police did nothing. Just let that prick Andy roam free. Now look what's happened. God I hope she's okay.' She looked out the window, holding the scrunched tissue to her nose.

As they drove west to the Bruce Highway the sky dimmed and a brush of colour streaked the western hills. Cameron reached over and patted Susie's leg.

'She's in good hands Suze.'

Susie nodded and sniffed. 'I'm so glad it was her leg. God I hate to think...'

'Did the police tell you much about what happened?' Cameron said. Susie blew her nose and took a deep breath.

'It was at the old flat where Andy used to live. Jasmine went there to see this Brad. Andy turned up and some guy with a gun was threatening him. Andy grabbed Jasmine as a human shield and the gunman fired.'

'So Jasmine was in the wrong place at the wrong time,' Cameron said. 'Did anyone else get hurt?'

'Yes. Andy's dead.' Susie paused. 'The police knew he was stalking her but what did they do? Nothing.'

'What about this Brad? Is he okay?'

'As far as I know.' They sat in silence for a while as they drove over the overpass bridge and headed north. 'Why didn't that Brad do something? He was there. He would have known Andy was trouble. Unless he's part of all the drug stuff that's been happening.'

'Maybe Jasmine can fill you in on more details. Don't stress yourself too much until you know more,' Cameron said. He had a calmness and sensibility about him that instantly eased her pain. And she sure needed that now.

They'd put Jasmine in the Intensive Care Unit while the doctors assessed her condition and planned their procedures. The unit was a capsule of beeping monitors and machines where patients teetered between life and death. Jasmine seemed to have tubes everywhere. Susie walked quickly to the bed and hugged her daughter.

'Jaz. Jaz. I'm here.'

Jasmine turned and smiled. 'It's okay Mum. It's just my leg. They can fix that,' she mumbled through the mask. She looked from Susie to Cameron.

'This is Cam. You remember, Adam's dad? He drove me here. I was a bit of a mess.'

Jasmine nodded. 'Hi. The doctors took x-rays. They might operate.' She looked past them. 'Here comes the doctor now.'

Dr Wallace was a short man with olive skin and black hair that was slicked neatly back. He introduced himself then said, 'Jasmine will need surgery to remove bullet fragments. Fortunately it missed bone but there has been some deep tissue damage.' He looked at Jasmine. 'She's young so she'll heal quickly. Probably on crutches for a while and may need physio. We won't know exactly until after the op.' He walked over to Jasmine. 'The nurses will prep you for theatre. You're doing fine.' He patted her hand then walked off checking his beeping pager.

Jasmine was wide-eyed. 'Crutches? Mum I don't want crutches. How will I drive? What about my job? The pelicans?'She started sniffling.

'It'll be okay. You heard the doctor. You'll heal in no time.'

Brad made his way to the ICU unit as directed by the nurse at the station on Level Three. She was a buxom woman with a starched face. She looked over her glasses and said, 'Only family are allowed in you know. And only two at a time.' Brad nodded and walked off.

As he reached the twin glass doors of the unit, a tall man and a woman with red puffy eyes walked out and stared at him. He felt clammy and scruffy in his crushed t-shirt.

'Are you Jasmine's mum?' he asked Susie.

'Yes. I'm Susie,' Susie said sharply.

He held out his hand. 'I'm Brad. Brad Nash, Jasmine's friend. How is she?' His hand stayed suspended so he dropped it quickly.

'You've got a hide,' Susie growled. 'How dare you turn up here.'

'What?' Brad mouthed. Looking from one to the other.

'It's your fault she's in here. You and your druggo friends.'
She stormed off, Cameron following like a confused puppy.
Then she spun around her face red and crumpled. 'Just keep
away from her. Do you hear me? Keep the fuck away.' An old
man poked his head out of a bathroom nearby and let his mouth
drop. The lift pinged and Cameron led her away.

Brad was glued to the spot. *God what was that?* It was pretty
clear he couldn't see Jasmine and he still didn't know how she
was. He rang the bell outside the ICU. After about a minute a
flustered nurse marched to the door.

'Yes?' she snapped.

'Jasmine...Jasmine Bennett. How is she?'

'Are you family?'

'No...I—'

'Sorry,' she said and closed the door.

Brad walked back along the cold, sterile corridor, his head
down. He waited for the lift and noticed the stiff nurse glaring at
him. His fingers itched. How he'd love to give her the finger.
Stupid old bitch.

*Why was Susie so aggro? Why does she think I'm into drugs?
I just wanted to see how Jaz was. I can't buy her flowers. All the
kiosks are shut. And we're off on the trawler tomorrow.* He ran
his hand through his hair. Then he had an idea.

He drove to his parents' home and strode in. His mum greeted him as she always did. She said John was in bed and that he'd settled down a lot now he was on medication. But he was spaced out most of the time and Cheryl was continuing to feel more and more trapped. She never said as much but Brad sensed it. He told his mum about the shooting.

'Oh my God Brad. You could have been killed.' Her hand went to her throat. 'I knew something was amiss. What time was it...when it happened?'

'About four I think.'

'That's spooky. You won't believe this. I have a Mary MacKillop medal in my jewellery box. I went into the bedroom around that time and it was on the floor. How would it get there?'

Brad was shaking his head, 'M-u-m.'

'No. It's true. I never took it out. It's always in the box.'

'Dad probably took it out.'

'What? No way. Why would he touch my jewellery?'

'You've got a good imagination,' he said shaking his head. 'Hey Mum. Could you do something for me tomorrow?' He asked Cheryl to get some flowers and send them to the hospital.

'She must be some girl if she's getting this treatment.'

'She's a good friend. I'm worried about her. That's all.'

'Okay. So what sort of flowers do you want?'

'You pick. You'll know what a girl likes.'

'And the card?'

'Yeah. I'll write what I want.' He grabbed a piece of paper and a pen from the bench near the phone and stared past his mother. He tapped the pen on the table. Then he wrote, "To Pelican Girl, Get well soon, Love Brad." He wasn't very good at drawing pelicans so he drew a little fish at the end.

He got up. 'It's been one hell of a day. I need to grab a beer. And Mum can I crash here? The cops won't let me back home just yet.'

'Sure that'll be fine. I'll send those flowers for you...and I'll pray to Mary MacKillop for your little Jasmine. Did you know that Mother Mary MacKillop will be Australia's first saint?'

'Thanks Mum,' Brad said smiling and shaking his head as he checked the fridge for beers.

Susie arrived back at the hospital early on Monday morning and headed to the ICU. She'd called last night after Jasmine's operation and they told her Jasmine was fine and resting comfortably. It was reasonably quiet in the wards at this hour as visitors wouldn't start arriving till about eleven. A woman in a pink uniform wheeled a tea trolley past and smiled. A young man on crutches was propping himself by the pay phone and gesturing with his hand as he talked.

'Oh Ms Bennett,' the nurse at the counter said. She pointed to a beautiful bunch of roses. 'These just arrived for Jasmine. She's not allowed to have flowers in ICU but perhaps you can give her the card. When she goes into the wards later this morning we'll bring the flowers in then.'

'Thanks,' Susie said. She took the card and walked off. She stopped when she opened it and her mouth dropped. She looked back at the nurses' station. No none was looking. She walked over and threw it in the bin.

Jasmine was asleep when Susie arrived but the nurse said she'd had a good night and the operation went well. She decided to call back later. She would finish her shopping, collect some things for Jasmine and bring Stephen along too.

TWENTY- TWO

Later that morning the wardsmen moved Jasmine into the general wards. It was a relief to now be in here not the ICU. It was for the dying or dead. Jasmine was still scared to close her eyes, the signal to her brain to launch into terror. It was always the same horrible nightmare, the burning agony in her leg, the load on her chest, the struggle for breath, the panic and screams cut off.

She plugged in the buds of her ipod, chose some Katy Perry music and wriggled down lower in the bed so her neck wasn't so stiff. The plastic underlay squished and puckered. Her right thigh was encased in bandages and her movement was restricted and awkward. At least the painkillers had kicked in and she felt only a little pain when she moved. There were three other beds in the room all occupied by older ladies. *God it's like a nursing home.* The old woman directly opposite her was on her back, mouth open and snoring raggedly. Beside her was a woman sleeping peacefully, her face visible above the sheet, a face as white and fragile as tissue paper. The other old lady wore a long pink dressing gown and kept muttering to herself. She was always on the move, wandering off to who knows where, and then protesting as the nurses brought her back and reprimanded her like a little child in trouble.

Jasmine's bed was near the window overlooking rainforest trees, and if she propped herself up she could see the tops of the buildings in the town. On the window ledge were several bouquets of flowers with cards attached. Jasmine loved the clutch of red roses and she wondered whose they were. None of her friends were allowed in the intensive care ward and they didn't allow flowers there either. But she knew they'd visit or contact her now she was out of danger. She looked at the tops of the trees rippling in the wind and thought about Brad. She was disappointed he hadn't left a note or message. Wouldn't you think he'd come to the hospital, find out how she was? She swallowed awkwardly to ease her dry and aching throat. Why did it all go so wrong? The tears welled up and she turned her head into the pillow and sobbed. She dried her eyes just as Susie and Stephen breezed in. Susie bent down and kissed her on the head.

'Hey,' she said. 'Look at you. You'll be up and about soon. The doctor said you're mending well. Are you in any pain?'

'No Mum. I'm fine.' She looked at Stephen standing awkwardly at the end of the bed. 'Hi Bro.' He moved forward and hugged her.

'You gave us a fright,' he said gruffly. He pulled away quickly and slunk at the end of the bed.

Susie rifled through her green shopping bag. 'I've brought your laptop, maybe you'll be allowed to use it, and some girlie magazines. Oh, and the girls sent this.' She handed over a handmade card from Megan and Amanda.

Jasmine smiled, read the card and reached for the laptop. 'Thanks Mum. Now I can go on Facebook and catch up. Any other messages?'

'I contacted the zoo and they said they'll keep your job, just get yourself better. And Christine at the Rescue Service wished you well. She said your special pelican friends will miss you.'

'Oh that's so nice,' Jasmine smiled. 'What about Brad? Did he contact you? Any messages?'

Susie shook her head and turned towards the window.

'Aren't they beautiful roses Mum? Someone in here is lucky.'

'Yes they are,' Susie said glancing around the room. 'But I don't think any of these old ladies are even aware of them. They seem like they're past caring too much.'

'Yeah I know it's sad. I definitely don't want to get old.'

After Susie and Stephen left, Jasmine opened her Facebook page and smiled as she scrolled through the messages. News travelled fast. She was aware of someone at the end of the bed. It was the frail lady in the dressing gown, a ghost in pink.

'They took my baby you know,' she said to Jasmine. Before Jasmine could respond a young nurse marched in and took the delicate woman gently by the arm.

'Come on now Beatrice. It's time for your tablet and a sleep.' She guided the old lady to her bed, gave her the medication and tucked her in. She walked over to check Jasmine's IV drip.

'How are you Jasmine?'

'Good. A lot better thanks.'

'My name's Renee. I'm the nurse on duty today. That must have been scary for you getting shot like that.'

'Yep it all happened so fast. It's like it was a dream...a bad dream.'

The nurse secured a fresh bag and tapped the drip line. She looked over at the flowers.

'I see you've got your roses,' she said.

'They're beautiful but I don't think they're mine.'

'Yes. Yes. They're yours. They arrived when you were in ICU. I gave the card to your mum. Didn't you get it yet?'

'No...I... maybe mum just forgot.'

'Well they might be from a secret admirer, who knows?' She patted the end of the bed and winked as she walked away.

Jasmine bit her lip. *Why didn't Mum give me the card? She wouldn't forget. She's too organised for that. Maybe they're from Brad. That would be so cool. But he wouldn't have had time to organise it. Who then? I guess I'll find out soon enough.*

Detectives Baker and Summers walked into the ward later that morning escorted by Renee.

'Jasmine,' she said, 'the detectives are here to ask questions. I've told them you are to be kept quiet and you need your rest.' She turned to the men. 'Not too long okay.' They nodded.

Jasmine took a deep breath. *When will this ever end? What now?*

After the pleasantries they drew the curtains and began their serious questioning.

'After the shooting we interviewed Bradley Nash. Now we want your recall of events,' Summers said, stroking his moustache.

'But Brad would have told you what happened.'

'We need as much information as we can get. This is serious stuff. A murder has occurred and you were lucky to escape a fatality as well. Surely you want us to get the people responsible.'

'Yes...I.' Jasmine took a deep breath and outlined what happened. It all seemed like some horror movie replaying in her head. She stopped several times for sips of water.

'Do you remember anything about the assailant? What he looked like? What he said?' Baker asked.

'It all happened so quickly. One minute we were at the door, the next I was on the floor in pain with Andy on top of me. I..my first reaction when I saw Andy coming towards us was one of panic, "What's he doing here?", and I remember the other guy was so close. I only saw his head briefly. He had a beanie pulled low and a beard...a wispy beard. I didn't have time to think. Andy grabbed me and spun me around...'

Nurse Renee poked her head through the curtain. 'Are you okay Jasmine?' Jasmine nodded. Renee addressed the two detectives, 'She needs her rest. Are you nearly done?'

The detectives nodded and finished off their questioning. 'Thanks Jasmine. You have been a big help. All the best,' Baker said and they left.

When Susie came back that night she brought up the subject of Jasmine's homecoming.

'Of course you'll come home with me, Jaz. No arguments.'

Jasmine started to protest.

'No Jaz. I'm taking some of my annual leave. You can't possibly look after yourself properly, and how would you get to the physio?'

Jasmine did not have the energy to argue.

'I have some other news,' Susie continued. 'I had an email from Petria. Guess what. She and her friend are coming up to the coast for a week and she wants to catch up.'

'Great. That'll be good. Did she say where she's staying?'

'She said her friend has family at Coolum so I guess they'll stay there.'

She paused and grabbed her bag. 'I have some more cards.' She handed them to Jasmine. There were cards from the zoo staff, the netball girls and Anita in Sydney. The last one was from

Christine and Phil at the Rescue Centre, a photo of the resident pelicans with well wishes on the back.

'What about the other card? The one that came with the roses?'

'What card?' Susie said as she zipped her bag up.

'The nurse Renee said she gave you the card from the roses.'

Susie shook her head. 'No. No other card. Must have been someone else.'

Why do I get the feeling she's lying? Why would she do that? Maybe the flowers are from Brad and she doesn't want me involved. I bet that's it.

Jasmine gazed at the roses. 'They are so nice. I hope it was Brad who sent them anyway.'

She glared at Susie's reddening face.

TWENTY- THREE

Brad had never experienced a week as long as this one. He couldn't stop thinking of Jasmine. How was she coping? Did she like the flowers?

He stood on the boat, his body dipping and swaying, the movement that was now so much a part of him, and willed the boat faster to the Mooloolaba coast. He grabbed his mobile and tried her number again, must be in range soon. Jasmine answered in an excited voice, 'Brad hey.'

'Hey. How are you?'

'Fine.Yeah, I'm okay. Got out of hospital yesterday. Don't like the crutches but hey?'

'What happened with the leg?'

Jasmine told him about the operation and the physio.

'I was glad to go home Brad. That place was like an oldies' home.'

'Did you get the flowers?'

'Um...I'm not sure. There were red roses with no card. Were they the ones?'

'I got Mum to send some so I hope they were nice, but I did write a card, sorry Babe.'

'Thanks Brad. They were really nice.'

'Hey this phone keeps cutting. I'll call round when I'm in and cleaned up okay.'

Jasmine held the phone to her chest. Her soul hummed. What was it about this guy that set her spinning? She felt she could trust him. And that was important after so many let-downs and betrayals. But a part of her was wary, a part of her held back...just a little.

When Brad's ute pulled up at the Golden Beach house Susie came out blazing.

'Jasmine's resting. It's not a good time.'

'Sorry,' Brad said, 'Jasmine said it was fine.'

'Well it's not. You need to leave,' she snapped.

Jasmine hobbled up behind her. 'Mum. God Mum. What's going on?' She pushed past Susie and nearly tripped on the stair, one crutch clattering to the ground. Brad rushed forward and grabbed her while Susie huffed back inside.

'Hey Brad,' Jasmine hugged him. 'Let's get out of here. Mum's being an idiot.'

They drove to the park and sat in the car overlooking the Passage. The sky was grey and scuds of light rain were sweeping across the channel.

'God I've missed this, the salty air, the water, the birds...' Jasmine sighed.

'And me,' Brad said his eyebrows raised.

Jasmine leant over and kissed him. 'Of course you too.' She paused and shifted her leg into a more comfortable position. 'Don't worry about Mum. She's just way too protective. Worried about the drug thing you know.'

'Yeah. Can't blame her really.'

'Brad, I need to leave. Go back to Buddina.I am being suffocated. You know she lied to me. That card that went missing...she had it...I know because the nurse told me she gave it to her while I was in ICU.'

'Well you can always move in with me,' Brad said reaching for her hand and giving it a gentle squeeze.

'Seriously. I don't think I could go back to that flat. Too many bad memories.' She looked through the misty windscreen and shivered. Droplets of rain were pooling and weaving their way downwards in delicate patterns.

'I understand totally. You must be freaked after what happened. I'm just so glad you're okay.'

'I can go back to Buddina. I'll be fine.'

Brad opened the door. 'Hey. I just remembered. I have something for you.' He jumped out and rummaged around in the back of the ute.

'Sorry about the wrapping,' he said as he presented her with a plastic bag. Droplets of rain beaded on his dark curls and a smile split his rugged face. Inside was one of the most beautiful shells Jasmine had ever seen. She gently pulled it out and turned it over, the light reflecting its apricot and pearly colours. She brushed her fingers over the intricate swirls and folds.

'Brad thanks. It's so cool. I love shells.'

'And before you say anything else, it was empty. No living creature was harmed in this exercise. We find quite a few shells in the nets, some empty, others occupied. I'm not sure what it is, but I think it's a type of trumpet shell.'

Their eyes sought each other and they kissed softly, warmly. Jasmine enveloped herself in the physical, the salt, the outdoor smell, the strength of him, the sea breath. For a moment she forgot her mangled leg and she curled her fingers around the shell wanting to hold this moment forever.

The mobile phone rang, and Jasmine frowned as she read the screen. 'Bloody Mum.'

Susie sat in the kitchen and pressed the phone harder to her ear willing an answer. It went to voice mail again. Why did the people you love have the capability to hurt you so much? She was only trying to help, do what most mothers would do. Why did she get kicked in the teeth? She sighed and rested her chin on her cupped hands. She stared at the sink piled with leaning plates and haphazard bowls. Just like me she thought, abandoned, ready to topple any minute.

She thought back to when she was sixteen, a bit younger than Jasmine, cooking and cleaning in this very kitchen. God she didn't even have a mother then. She and her sister had to take over where their mother had left off. That's what their dad expected. He was from the old school of belief that women were there to look after the men, do the cooking, cleaning, fussing. After her mum died, her father wrapped himself up in his selfish, sorrowful blanket, blind to the fact that others missed her too. She soldiered on, suppressing thoughts and burying the pain. Life was never the same after her mother died and Susie knew she had to leave or she'd die too, right along with her. She was always searching for nurturing in her relationships, and she realised now that no one could meet that need. No one could fill the hole her mother left. She was determined to make it on her own, be her own person, and if she had any kids she'd make sure they were looked after and loved totally.

But it was a tough world out there and she made mistakes along the way. How can you protect your kids from the hurts, the same mistakes? Sometimes it all seemed too hard.

Susie's car had gone when Jasmine and Brad returned from the park. Jasmine was pleased in a way as she didn't want to deal with more arguments. Brad helped her out so she could collect her things and they could head back to Buddina. She left a quick note for Susie.

Brad dropped her off and said he'd see her tomorrow for her physio. He really wanted to stay but Megan was probably there and he wanted to visit his mum. He didn't want to rush things and he sensed Jasmine was a bit touchy.

On the way to his mum's the mobile rang. He pulled over and answered.

'Brad,' Cheryl choked. 'You'd better come home quick.'

'Mum...What---'

'Just come home. I can't talk on the phone.'

Brad swung back onto the motorway and ran his hand through his hair. *What now? What had the stupid prick done now? They should lock him up and throw away the key. The selfish bastard.*

A police car was outside the house. *Shit.* His mum was on the lounge chair being comforted by a female police officer while the male officer stood awkwardly with his hat in his hands. When they saw Brad, they both moved to the door, offering apologies, nodding and then slipping away. Brad stood still, confused, then rushed to his mum.

'What Mum? What's happened?' But part of him really knew.

Cheryl wiped her nose and looked up, her face blotched and ravaged.

'He's gone Brad. He killed himself.' She clutched at him and sobbed. He held her frail trembling body and kissed her head. What could he say? His throat had seized up. He'd wished for this all along hadn't he? Now the bastard could be at peace...or could he?

'Where Mum? When ?'

'This morning. Point Cartwright. He drove to the park...and he went up there, you know the cliff on the headland. He jumped.'

'God how awful,' Brad mumbled.

Cheryl stared ahead and twisted her hands. 'I guess he has some kind of peace now. He suffered so much over the years.'

What about us? Didn't we suffer too? What sort of life did she have living with that maniac?

Brad got up. 'I'll make you a cuppa,' he said. He knew now it would be full on. He'd have to inform relatives and arrange the funeral. He called Jasmine.

'I'm so sorry,' she said. 'How can I help?'

'I'll call over tonight if that's okay. I'll need a shoulder to lean on.'

Later that night Brad fell into Jasmine's arms and they held each other so tightly that neither wanted to let go. Megan had just left on her trip to Melbourne so they had the unit to themselves. Jasmine whispered into Brad's ear, her mouth brushing the dark curls on his neck. She led him down the hall to her room and they curled up on the bed together. No words were needed. They held each other, finding comfort in the touch, the breathing, the warmth. This was summer, this was song, this was refuge. Slowly the clothes came off and they savoured each other's bodies. A soft light crept in from the street lamp, angling through the curtain while waves crashed and slapped on the nearby beach. But they could have been on another planet. Jasmine quivered like a baby bird, arching her body and crying out as Brad powered and exploded like the churning ocean waves outside.

TWENTY- FOUR

As the coffin was lowered into the ground, Brad stood transfixed. The casket was draped with an Australian flag and his dad's digger's hat was sitting mournfully on top. He held Cheryl's shaking body and rubbed his hand up and down her arm. Now she was free. Free of living with a time bomb. But she wouldn't see it that way. She was obviously shattered, but he knew she'd be okay after time, with his support and that of her friends and work colleagues, her sister, and of course her church. It was her faith that kept her going she said. And she'd certainly done God's work, a saint that's what she was. She'd always made excuses for his dad's erratic behaviour and cutting comments, but Brad was less forgiving. It took a long time to accept things, to move on. The put-downs and outbursts of emotional abuse were grinding and hurtful.

He looked across the grave at the regimental line of solemn men, Vietnam Veterans, heads bowed in silence, all kitted out with their suits and medals, and he felt like screaming at them. They were living a lie. They'd been duped. Couldn't they see that? How many more of them would end up in the coffin prematurely like his dad? What a waste, the senselessness of war. He shook his head as his eyes smarted.

The past days had been hectic and emotional with relatives arriving and funerals plans to be made. He hadn't been able to see Jasmine much but he knew her thoughts were with him. She'd offered to come but he'd declined. This wasn't a place for her, and she'd feel awkward. She was so special to him that just thinking about her made him warm inside. He had to stop himself from reliving their intimate moments, the touch of her velvet skin, her sweet breath, the lingering perfume that sent his senses racing. But she had her own problems right now, a stiff and painful leg, an overbearing mother, the drug charge. And the sister she didn't know existed, she'd just arrived. It was full on.

Jasmine had a phone call from Geoff Benito the solicitor her mum had arranged to represent her with the drug charge. He told her that the police had arrested the two people involved in her attack, and that this had played a crucial part in breaking up some major drug trade activities.

'But like I said before you were involved with this Andy Pascoe, you were his girlfriend. They will allege you were aware of his trafficking activities, even participating in it. We have to prove that you were an innocent party in this,' he said.

'I can't believe I was so naive,' Jasmine said.

'I will need all the information you can give me, Jasmine. Can I make a time to see you and we can go over a few things?'

After arranging a time to meet Mr Benito, Jasmine called her mum to tell her about the meeting with Petria. There was no answer again. She hadn't been able to contact Susie since she left that day with Brad. Maybe her mum was in a huff. She tried Stephen's phone and he told her Susie had gone away for a few days with Cameron.

'Where to?' Jasmine asked.

'How would I know?' Stephen grumbled.

Jasmine shrugged. This was not like her mum. She didn't just up and go off with some man. *But maybe she knows him better than I think. And I wonder why she's not answering. Pissed off with me probably.*

Petria arrived at the unit in her usual bubbly, eccentric way. She was accompanied by another young, slim girl who was more conservatively dressed, figure-hugging jeans and white shirt. She was pale with fine features, long blonde hair flowing freely.

She had a timid smile and stunning eyes the colour of autumn leaves.

'It's so cool to see you again Jasmine,' Petria gushed. She introduced her friend. 'This is Amy. We've been friends for ages.'

Jasmine greeted them both and limped inside.

'I can't believe what happened to you Girl,' Petria said. 'Sit down and I'll make the coffee.'

'Yep. It was pretty weird. I still have nightmares.'

'Poor love. Did they get the bad guys?'

'Yes. They've been arrested. Seems like they were part of a drug ring.'

'Nasty. Anyway tell me what else has been happening. Your job? Love life?' She smiled.

Jasmine talked a little about the photo job. 'You must go to the zoo while you're here. Have you guys been to the coast before?' They both nodded.

'Yeah we have. Amy's family live at Coolum so we try to come up when we can.'

'What about you Amy? What do you do?' Jasmine asked.

'I work with Petria at the theatre. I help in the costuming department,' Amy said softly.

'That must be so cool. What sort of costumes are you doing now?'

'Well we just got a contract to do work for a new musical show about witches so some of those costumes are going to be fun.' Amy twisted some hair strands in her hand as she spoke.

Petria looked around. 'Anyone else live here?'

'Megan. She's away for a few days.'

'How do you manage on your own? You know with the busted leg and everything?' Petria asked.

'Well it's a lot better now. But I can't drive yet so my friend Brad helps me out.'

'And you've got Susie too. Hey couldn't she make it?'

'No.'

Petria stood and took the cups to the sink. 'You know Jasmine you should come to Sydney. There are heaps of jobs there.'

'I'd like to come again. I miss my old friends but I'm happy here. Brad's talking about going to the mines near Mackay.I might even go up there myself. Who knows?'

Petria's eyebrows shot up. 'Wo. This Brad must be some guy.' She put her hands on her hips. Jasmine's face coloured.

'Well we've only just got together, but he's really nice. Pretty hot actually.' They all smiled.

'We have some news for you,' Petria said as she walked over to Amy. She wrapped her arms around her friend and said, 'We are getting married...in September. We'd love you to come.'

Jasmine swallowed hard and pushed her chair back. This was some surprise.

'Congratulations. I'm so happy for you,' Jasmine said as she moved towards them, arms outstretched.

'Group hug,' she said and they all laughed in their circled embrace.

TWENTY- FIVE

As the winter months approached, Jasmine was able to at last get reprieve from the past months of turmoil. It was time to sit back and take a deep breath. She felt like her boat, having weathered the storms, was now in calm waters and she could journey on with renewed hope. The horizon beckoned with optimism, a new future. She was enjoying time spent with Brad and they were growing closer every day.

When Brad had mentioned earlier about going to the mines in Central Queensland, Jasmine's heart sank. *Why did things like this happen to me? We've only just started. We have something special here. I want so much to make something of my life, pursue my dreams. And I want to be with Brad.*

Just lately he had suggested that she come too. 'There's a wildlife park in Mackay,' he'd said. 'You could check it out.

See if there are any jobs. And you could still do your study externally,' he continued.

She'd tossed the ideas around in her head, analysing the pros and cons. It would be a change and wasn't this what she needed? She'd still be able to come back to Caloundra for visits. At least she wouldn't be overseas. The coal mine was two hour's drive from Mackay so Brad had suggested they rent a unit near the beach and he would stay in the miners' accommodation some week nights. It meant she'd be on her own at times but she felt she could cope, keeping busy with her studies and painting.

While her leg was healing she'd picked up the brush again and completed some small pelican and beach paintings. They'd been a hit at the markets so she felt she could still be a help for the Rescue Centre. Christine said that she should think about writing and illustrating a children's book about pelicans. It would be popular with the kids and tourists and raise the awareness of young people. That would be an interesting project she thought. She could see herself as a book illustrator, but she'd have to get help or direction with the writing side of it. But who knows where all that might lead?

Her mind was racing as she started walking towards the canal. She took some photos across the aqua water of the coloured yachts moored to the pylons. That would make a great pastel picture. There didn't seem to be as many pelicans here at Buddina but she'd spotted a few around the marina waiting for the fish handouts from the tourist boat. The boat came by at the same time every morning and the pelican feeding was one of its main attractions. She'd seen and heard black cockatoos too which loved feasting on the banksia seeds, and often she saw a majestic osprey in the high branches of the older skeletal casuarina trees. She'd miss all of this, but Mackay would have its beaches and wildlife. She'd heard about Eungella National Park with its rainforest and wildlife, and Mackay was the gateway to many islands and reefs. Brad was mad keen to go out reef fishing, and it was regarded as fisherman paradise up there.

She bit her lip and sighed. *Would Brad really want me up there? What if it didn't work out?* She knew what her mother would say. And she'd been burnt before, rushing in head on. There was a strong connection with Brad though, and she found a part of her was missing when he was not around. They'd spent a lot of time together in the past months when they'd both been emotionally tested. If he could put up with her girlie moods and quirky artistic drive, then she could overlook his bossiness and the fact that he often drank too much. She felt alive when she was with him, drawn to his solidarity, his loyalty, the mystery of his inner sensitivity.

Jasmine's lawyer Mr Benito had sufficient evidence to convince the magistrate that Jasmine was an innocent party in the drug activities, and she was let off on a good behaviour bond. She had a visit from the detectives after she left hospital and they told her how she could apply for compensation as a victim of crime. They told her how the drug ring had been disabled and the bikie and his blonde charged. 'Those drug gangs are deadly. Be a bit more careful Jasmine. Choose your friends wisely,' Detective Brady had said.

Jasmine was so relieved when the court hearing was all over. Her leg was healing well and she could get on with her life. What had her horoscope said? "There will be emotional times, but put these behind you. The following months will see recovery and matters of the heart will bloom. Travel is likely." She felt content knowing that she was making progress with her goals; study, a job where she could help the animals, and love. It all looked so promising. And her mum was so settled now. She'd felt guilty at first moving out of home, but look what happened. Cameron and Susie were now an item and Jasmine had never seen her mum look so happy. Even Stephen was making moves. He'd been offered a traineeship at the local surf shop. At first he would be in charge of the "Learn to Surf" classes and then the boss said he could progress in the business, doing sales and then management. It was a great opportunity.

After a few months of planning, scanning the internet and networking, Jasmine and Brad decided that he would go up to the mines first, settle in and see if he liked it. Jasmine could come up for weekends occasionally, and he would have time off too, so they could see how that worked. She was back at her zoo job and decided to hang in there till things sorted out. It would be tough but they were both willing to try it.

'Why would you want to go all the way up there?' Susie said when Jasmine returned home from Buddina for a visit. Things were still a bit strained between them. 'You hardly know the guy.'

'Mum it feels right. I love Brad....and it will be a good experience moving to a new place, working there.'

'Well you thought you loved that Andy too and look what happened.' Susie put the steaming coffees on the table. 'Would you like a biscuit or muffin?'

'I'd love a muffin, I miss home cooking.' She breathed in the coffee aroma and sighed. Coffee always tasted better at home.

'Mum what about Cameron? What's happening there?'

Susie looked up with a smile. 'He's just a very good friend. That's all,' she muttered, then took a bite of muffin.

'You tell me to take things slowly.'

'I haven't rushed into anything. Cam's a nice guy. We have a lot in common.'

'Then why can't you see why I want to do this?'

'You're young,' Susie said staring past Jasmine to the window. 'I know what I was like at your age.'

Jasmine put her mug down. 'I am not you Mum. And anyway I have to learn by my own mistakes don't I?'

'I don't want you hurt that's all.' They sat in their own silences for a while. Jasmine's mobile beeped, a new message.

'I have sum gr8 news when will u b bk?'

Jasmine replied, drank the dregs of her coffee and said goodbye to Susie.

Brad was waiting for her at Buddina his face beaming. As she got out of her car he ran over, swept her off her feet and twirled her around. Jasmine screamed and nearly lost her balance when he deposited her on the footpath. He grabbed her face in his hands.

'Babe. You will never ever guess what.' His face was red, ready to burst.

Jasmine mouthed, 'What?'

'At the pub. You know how they have competitions? When you buy beer you can enter them?' Jasmine nodded. Brad dropped his hands and yelled. 'I won. I won. I won a trip to the Greek Islands.' He grabbed Jasmine again. 'It's for a week and it's for two people. You and me Babe.' They both laughed and danced around in a circle.

When their state of euphoria wore off a little, they decided to find out about the places they'd visit. The cruise went to three of the main islands, Mykonos, Rhodes and Santorini.

'I can't believe it,' Jasmine said. 'The Greek Islands. How romantic. I remember the movie "Mamma Mia". It was set on one of the islands. I just love that movie and the scenery is spectacular.

When she googled "Mykonos" she discovered something special.

'Hey Brad look at this. They say that Mykonos has some resident pelicans and there's a story about them.'

Brad rolled his eyes. 'Can't we get away from those bloody birds?' he joked. Jasmine thumped his arm.

'Listen. There are several sites here which say that in the 1950s a fisherman discovered an injured pelican and brought him back to Mykonos where he cared for him. The pelican followed the fisherman everywhere and decided to make the island his home. The locals called him Petros. He became the island's mascot, a tourist attraction. When he died thirty years later the island residents were devastated so three pelicans were donated to them; Irene, Nickolas and another Petros. And look Brad there are photos and videos.' Brad came over and leaned on the back of the chair.

'Petros doesn't look like our pelicans. He's all white, no it's a pinkish white.' He bent down and kissed her on the lips. 'It will be the best time Babe,' he said.

They decided to take the holiday in August before moving and settling into new jobs. So there were still a few months ahead to settle down, save up some spending money and plan their trip. It felt like a whirlwind, scary but exciting just the same. *This holiday will be a big test. It will either make us or break us Jasmine thought.* Her friends were supportive. 'Hey follow your heart. We are so-o jealous,' Amanda had said.

The islands were everything they'd imagined and more. Santorini, an old volcano, was fascinating with its blue-white buildings clinging to the cliffs like icing dribbling on top of a cake, and the wonky donkeys zig-zagging up the slopes carrying travellers from the port at the bottom to the little village of Fira at the top. The village was a network of narrow paved alleyways and steep stairs. They dined in a small restaurant high above the precipice, and gazed dreamily over the deep blue waters of the caldera where the huge anchored cruise ships looked like toys way below them.

Rhodes' old town was enclosed in castle walls, a place full of history and classical medieval monuments. Jasmine was fascinated by the jewellery shops and the amazing variety of leather goods.

And then there was Mykonos. A turquoise sea, white-washed buildings, a maze of twisting laneways, quaint cafes, tiny tourist shops, windmills. It didn't take Jasmine long to find Petros posing like a celebrity on the esplanade. She took lots of photos and brushed his long pink feathers.

Because it was the northern summer, the place was crawling with tourists and the shop owners were doing a brisk trade. In one shop Jasmine spotted some small, rectangular canvas paintings depicting beach and street scenes in the typical blues and whites of Greece. When she looked closely she could see how cleverly and deftly the artist had used the palette knife and how the shadows and highlights were so expertly done with complementary colours.

'I have to get a couple of these,' she said. 'Our mums will love them.' Brad managed to haggle the little Greek man who obliged with a gappy smile, then proceeded to follow them out of the shop.

'Here you like coasters too?' He pushed the box towards them.

'No thanks. We're right,' Jasmine and Brad said as they waved and jostled their way out into the brilliant sunshine.

They found a table in the beachside cafe right beside the little shop. Most of the tables were under shady striped awnings out in the fresh air overlooking the small harbour. Colourful boats bobbed on the water and Jasmine could see Petros waddling over the pebbled beach away from the tourists gathered at the water fountain. He was obviously tired of posing for the tourist photos. Greek salad never tasted so good; chunky sun-ripened tomatoes, olives, red onion, crispy cucumber, topped with a slab of rich fetta cheese. And added to this, red wine and home-baked bread dipped in olive oil. Greek mandolin music danced through the cafe and floated above them.

'I could get up right now and dance around to that music,' Jasmine giggled.

'Why don't you?' Brad said rising from his chair.

Jasmine looked embarrassed and covered her face. 'No. Sit down Brad,' she whispered.

He held out his hand and then dragged her to a space at the edge of the cafe. And they danced and twirled while the patrons started clapping, a few at first, then everyone cheered and clapped. When they stopped Brad kissed her passionately and the crowd loved that even more.

He scooped her up in his strong arms and called out. 'We're getting married.' The crowd erupted.

'What?' Jasmine mouthed when he finally put her down. She frowned, gulped and repeated, 'What? What?'

He held her out in front of him, tears glistening in his eyes.

'Pelican girl I love you. Will you marry me?' There was silence and Jasmine could feel a hundred pairs of eyes boring into her. She glanced around at the faces of anticipation in the cafe. She looked over at Petros who had ambled up from the sand. He nodded his head and snapped his scissor bill open and shut. She turned to Brad her mouth dry and her throat in spasm.

'Yes. Yes. I will.' The cheers and applause rang out and the mandolin started up again as Brad and Jasmine clung together.

The story of their journey as single people had started with pelicans, and now it had ended with a pelican, a very special pelican.